**"If you don't sta**

**my way for the n**

**I'm going to take**

**me five years ago."**

The growled ultimatum was a promise, not a threat. But the intent in Jared's eyes and the flood of moisture between her thighs jerked Katie out of the sensual trance. Her flight instinct finally kicked in.

Fumbling to put the vase on the edge of the counter, she turned and fled.

She raced to her room and shut the door. Her whole body shook. Sinking to the floor, her back hit the wall with a thud as she pressed her forehead to her knees and tried to make sense of the emotions, the needs careening through her system.

How could she be so enthralled by this man? She'd kissed other men—before and since she'd kissed Jared Caine. But no man had ever had the ability to reach inside her and yank out that part of herself she'd kept hidden for so long. And the realization terrified her.

*USA TODAY* bestselling author **Heidi Rice** lives in London, England. She is married with two teenage sons—which gives her rather too much of an insight into the male psyche—and also works as a film journalist. She adores her job, which involves getting swept up in a world of high emotions; sensual excitement; funny, feisty women; sexy tortured men; and glamorous locations where laundry doesn't exist. Once she turns off her computer, she often does chores—usually involving laundry!

**Books by Heidi Rice**

**Harlequin Presents**

*The Virgin's Shock Baby*
*Vows They Can't Escape*

**Harlequin KISS**

*Beach Bar Baby*
*Maid of Dishonor*
*Too Close for Comfort*

Visit the Author Profile page
at Harlequin.com for more titles.

# CAPTIVE AT HER ENEMY'S COMMAND

Recycling programs for this product may not exist in your area.

ISBN-13: 978-1-335-41930-9

Captive at Her Enemy's Command

First North American publication 2018



This edition published by arrangement with Harlequin Books S.A.

For questions and comments about the quality of this book, please contact us at CustomerService@Harlequin.com.

Printed in U.S.A.

# CAPTIVE AT HER ENEMY'S COMMAND

To Rob; thanks for the trip to Capri.
Best inspiration ever!

# PROLOGUE

*THIS IS YOUR MOMENT. Don't mess it up.*

Katie Whittaker jammed her ear against the living room door, straining to hear Jared Caine's voice through the wood as he talked on his cell phone. Her heartbeat thumped her throat in heavy staccato punches.

"Lloyd Whittaker's arraignment hearing is tomorrow. I've got Danners and Ramirez escorting her to the courthouse to testify. She's holding up okay. She's not great at taking orders, but she's pretty spunky for a kid whose old man beat up her sister right in front of her."

*A kid?*

Heat exploded in her cheeks like a mushroom cloud—and her heart shrank in her chest.

She was nineteen. She wasn't a kid. Not anymore. Not after what had happened two weeks ago.

A shudder reverberated down her spine at the memory of her sister Megan's cries for help muffled by another door.

*Don't think about that now.*

Megan was safe now in Italy with Dario De Rossi—the billionaire who had rescued her sister the night Lloyd Whittaker had gone rogue. The man Megan was going to marry.

Katie swallowed past the bubble of panic—and loneliness.

Megan deserved to be happy. Megan deserved to be the Whittaker sister having lots of hot sex on a private island in Italy with her handsome billionaire fiancé—because she'd stood up to their father, and taken the brunt of his anger, while Katie, as usual, had gotten off scot-free. Because, instead of busting down the door and saving Megan herself, Katie had run away and got Dario De Rossi to do the job for her.

Was that why Jared Caine—the security expert Dario had asked to look out for her—thought she was still a kid? Did he know what a coward she'd been?

Ever since their first meeting when Dario had introduced her to his friend Jared—and he'd clasped her fingers in a strong, unyielding grip that had sent five hundred volts of electrical energy zipping and zinging up her arm—she'd wanted him to like her. But everything she'd done to attract his attention, to get him to notice her, had backfired.

When she'd followed his instructions to the letter, he'd simply stopped coming around, leaving his men to watch over her. And, when she'd argued with his orders, instead of him realizing she was too old to be treated like a child he'd become even more detached, even more patronizing, listening patiently to all her concerns then telling her what to do anyway.

But tonight all that was going to change. She was going to show Jared she wasn't that frightened kid who had run out on her own sister. She was going to show him the real Katie. Show him that she could be strong, smart and brave just like Megan. When she put her mind to it.

Panic wrestled with the mac and cheese she'd had for dinner.

*All you have to do is show him who you really are.*

She clasped the handle and willed herself to open the door.

*"You know what you are, Katie? You're just like your mother."*

Lloyd Whittaker's oft-repeated observation whispered across her consciousness—insidious and destructive—and her fingers clenched on the polished glass handle.

*It's not true.*

She was nothing like Alexis Whittaker. The woman who had let down everyone who loved her. Megan had told her as much over years and years, whenever Lloyd Whittaker had accused Katie of being reckless and stupid and shallow. And, anyway, they'd discovered two weeks ago that Lloyd Whittaker wasn't even their biological father. He'd just pretended to be for years so he could steal money from their trust fund. So what did he know?

The latch clicked and Katie stepped into the room. The breath she'd been holding gushed out as Jared's gaze rose from his cell phone. He stood in the window alcove, silhouetted by the street lamp outside, his tall, broad-shouldered frame on instant alert.

"Katherine? Is there a problem?" He tucked his cell phone into the back pocket of his pants. The intensity of his gaze as he studied her had warmth blooming in her stomach, and it gave her the courage to walk across the room.

She loved the way he looked at her, as if she was the only person he could see. The only person who mattered in that instant. No one had ever looked at her with that much concentration before. Not even Megan.

She forced herself to keep on going, her bare feet making no sound on the rug.

"Maybe," she said, past lungs clamped in a vice.

"What is it?" She heard the concern. Need rolled through her and her heart pumped so fast she could hear it thundering in her ears.

He did care, behind that wall of detachment, that veneer of professionalism.

She didn't stop until she reached the alcove—and stood close enough to him to absorb the harsh beauty of his rough-hewn features. She let her gaze drift over the intriguing scar which bisected his upper lip, the closely cropped US Marine-style hair, which made him look fierce enough to wipe out a Taliban stronghold single-handed, the sensual mouth that never quite cracked a smile and the defined muscles on his arms and shoulders stretching the seams of the tailored white shirt.

At five foot eight she had always felt too tall, but Jared Caine had to bend his head to meet her gaze. The evidence of his height sent the whisper of sensation shuddering downward. And the vice around her lungs tightened.

"Why don't you ever call me Katie?" she asked.

His gaze remained steady, the blue of his irises so deep and true in the light from the street, she felt herself drowning in them. Every inch of her skin prickled with reaction. The awareness of him was so strong, the muscles in her belly liquefied.

A muscle twitched in the stubble on his cheek. And his gaze flicked down.

A startling heat swept through her, driven by the five hundred volts she remembered from the only time she'd been able to touch him. But they weren't touching now. The brushed cotton of her sleep T-shirt rasped across her nipples like sandpaper and tightened them into hard, rigid peaks.

She crossed her arms over her chest, mortified that she hadn't worn a bra. Could he see the effect he was having on her? Was that a good thing or a bad thing?

He gave a sigh. "Go to bed, Katherine," he said at last, his voice gruff.

"I don't want to go to bed. I want to stay here with you," she said, getting fixated on his lips and the white scar that bisected the bow on top. What would it feel like to kiss him? To have him kiss her back? Anticipation made her feel almost giddy.

"That's not a good idea." His voice was so husky

now she could feel it rumble between her legs, reverberating in the spot she stroked in bed at night while she was thinking about him.

"Why not?" Her heart fluttered in her chest when his brows lowered. She could smell him, soap and musk. The tense muscle in his cheek jerked.

"I think you know why."

It was all the encouragement she needed. He wasn't looking at her as if she was a kid anymore. Endorphins careered through her system, obliterating every thought but one.

*Just do it, already. Kiss him.*

Rising on tiptoes, she flung her arms around his neck. Her tender breasts flattened against rigid muscles as she pressed her lips to his.

Peppermint-flavored breath brushed her burning cheeks as he grunted a curse word. But his labored breathing yanked at the sweet spot between her legs. Greedy for more, she licked at the scar, and scraped her fingernails through the soft bristles of hair at his nape. His lips opened and her tongue delved into the recesses of his mouth. Harsh and insistent, she gathered his taste like a starving person—the delicious tang of peppermint and desire.

Big hands grasped her waist as reaction shuddered through him. And his long fingers fisted in the thin cotton of her T-shirt. Fierce joy blossomed inside her as his tongue tangled with hers—dominant and demanding. The vicious heat throbbed, making the sweet spot swell.

But before she could grab hold of the euphoria,

before she could bask in the hot glow, he reared back and ripped his mouth away.

"Damn it, Katherine. Stop it." Grasping her wrists in an iron grip, he thrust her hands down and shoved her back.

His crystal-blue eyes were like chips of ice in that lean, masculine face. "What kind of a game do you think you're playing?" The harsh words slashed through the euphoria like a machete.

"I'm sorry," she blurted out. "I thought..."

"What? That I wanted you to kiss me?" The sharp tone sliced to the bone. "I don't."

She hunched her shoulders. Dragging her wrists free of his grip, she clasped her arms around her waist, trying to hold the agony of his rejection inside. Why did everyone always reject her in the end? Why had she always been so unworthy of love?

She wanted to disappear. To fold herself up so small no one could ever see her again. Especially when the one question she'd never been able to ask before burst out of her mouth.

"Why not?"

He thrust his fingers through his hair, looking tense, and more agitated than she had ever seen him. "Because you're just a kid," he said, but his voice had softened. "And I don't kiss kids."

She forced her face up, her humiliation beyond bearing.

He looked shocked and angry and a strangled laugh burst out of her mouth—the hysteria going some way to mask the hurt.

She had wanted to get a reaction out of Jared Caine, and now she had. Unfortunately, it was the wrong one.

His eyebrow shot up his forehead. "You think this is funny?" he snapped.

It wasn't—in fact it was easily one of the least funny moments of her entire life—but she could never let him know that.

"I think it's hilarious," she lied as she shoved her chin out and stiffened her spine, adopting the pose she had used so often before when sassing Lloyd Whittaker to disguise the pain of his rejections.

"You spoiled brat." Caine's face hardened. "You try a stunt like that again and I'll put you over my knee and spank you myself. I don't care whose damn sister you are."

"Don't worry, I won't," she shot back. "You're not even any good at it."

It wasn't true, of course. For that brief moment of bliss his lips had felt so firm, so sure, so perfect.

Swinging round, she raced out of the room and slammed the door.

But, as fast as she ran, she couldn't escape the misery spreading through her like a virus.

Hitting her bed, she shoved her head under her pillow to muffle the wrenching sobs that poured out.

She didn't want him to hear her crying.

But as the anguish slammed into her full force, it brought with it the cruel punch of memory. And the sounds of her father's ranting—the words he'd shouted at Megan while he'd beat her sister with a belt.

*"You're just like her, both of you. No loyalty, no respect. Both little whores."*

Katie curled in on herself, trying to hold back the images which had tormented her for two long weeks.

But they played in her mind like a horror movie: Megan's broken body curled on the floor, her arms flung over her head, the vivid welts on her shoulder blades accompanied by their father's taunts and the sickening thud of leather hitting bone.

Katie gulped in breaths, the sobs so violent they wracked her whole body.

But the sweet spot between her legs still ached to be touched, her lips still felt tender and her cheeks still stung from the rasp of Caine's jaw.

And the hideous truth kept repeating inside her head, over and over and over again.

Lloyd Whittaker had been wrong about Megan, punishing her for something their mother had done, but he had always been right about her.

And now Jared Caine knew it too.

# CHAPTER ONE

*Five years later, the Amalfi Coast, Italy*

*PLEASE DON'T DIE...please don't die.*

Katie prayed for all she was worth, but the god of smartphone batteries wasn't listening because the phone screen cut to black.

She whimpered and stopped walking—or rather hobbling—along the narrow farm road as it dawned on her that having had most of her worldly possessions snatched by a couple of teenage sneak thieves wasn't the worst thing that could happen to her today.

The sun had sunk another inch toward the horizon, lengthening the shadows over the landscape of lemon and orange groves perched on the hillside.

She had been blown away by the wonder of the view at dawn that morning when she'd ventured down the deserted track on her second-hand Vespa to find a secluded cove to paint. But anxiety rose like a wave to add to her exhaustion now. In an hour, two at the most, it would be pitch-dark. And she would be stranded miles from the nearest town with no transport, no money, no means of communication, no luggage—she peered down at her bare legs and feet, covered in a layer of dirt that reached her knees—and no shoes.

Resisting the urge to hurl the offending phone—which hadn't had a signal for hours—onto the rocks below, she shoved it into the pocket of her shorts.

How ironic that three months ago when she'd first arrived at Charles de Gaulle airport from New York with nothing but a backpack, the beautiful mahogany box of art supplies Megan had given her and her passport, the whole point had been to travel light. To support herself and spend some time on her own. To prove to herself and everyone else that she could be more than a serial screw-up or microcelebrity click bait.

On her first night in Paris, in a little hostel near the Bastille, she'd been terrified, but over the weeks and months since, she'd started to find something in Europe she'd never had in the US. Anonymity and hard work had finally given her the time and space she needed to grow up.

She'd made new friends—waiting tables in a brasserie in the Marais, making beds in a hotel near St Mark's Square and hiking thirty miles on the Camino Real—but in the last month she had started to really appreciate her own company. She'd even managed to start earning real cash doing watercolor landscapes she posted each week to a gallery in Florence.

She hefted the box under her arm, which had begun to feel as if it weighed several tons about a mile and ten thousand blisters ago. At least she still had her paints.

But she'd discovered today she had a lot to learn about personal safety and not being an easy mark. If only she'd been less absorbed in her watercolor of the cove and more alert when Pinky and Perky had appeared from nowhere, maybe they wouldn't have managed to hot-wire her scooter, wrestle her pack off her and then disappear in a cloud of dust and victorious whoops in the space of approximately twenty-five seconds.

*How come I always have to learn everything the hard way?*

She forced herself to keep going, even though her feet hurt from tiptoeing over the rocky path and her head was pounding as if someone had sideswiped her with her own pack. Probably because they had.

She tested the knot forming on her forehead with her fingertips.

If she ever caught up with Pinky and Perky, she was going to stab them both through the heart with a well-sharpened artist's pencil. And then roast them like bacon.

The hum of an engine cut into her barbeque fantasies and a low-slung car appeared ahead of her, driving past the ruins of an old farmhouse. Or rather bouncing toward her on the uneven track.

Her breath gushed out, the wave of relief so extreme she felt nauseous. Maybe she could hitch a ride to Sorrento.

The sleek convertible was brand new and expensive. Apprehension cut off her optimism. What was this guy doing destroying his suspension on a farm track?

She brushed her hair over the bruising on her forehead and gripped the box in her arms, prepared to use it as a lethal weapon if her rescuer turned out to have the same moral compass as Pinky and Perky.

The car stopped a few yards ahead and a man stepped out. With the sun sinking, it was hard to make out more than a silhouette. But her heartbeat began to kick her ribs like a carthorse as he strolled toward her. His stride, leisurely and yet filled with purpose, looked familiar. And not in a good way.

*Jared Caine? How the hell...?*

The man stopped in front of her and his head dipped, as if he were checking her over.

The hum that started low in her abdomen was also disturbingly familiar.

*It can't be Caine. I must be hallucinating. Or seriously concussed. Or both.*

"Hello, Katherine." The deep voice, curt and businesslike, hauled her back to one of the lowest points in her life—even lower than this one, and that was saying something.

"What are you doing here?" she managed, still hoping she'd conjured him up from the depths of her sunstroke.

But then the shifting sunset glinted off the dark waves of his hair—no longer subdued by the buzz cut of five years ago—and cast a golden glow over his rugged features for the first time. A jolt of awareness hit her insides like a lightning strike, frying the tight knots of tension in her gut.

"Rescuing you," he said, with only the barest hint of sarcasm. "Now, get in the car before you fall on your face."

Jared Caine watched the horrified shock widen Katherine Whittaker's emerald-green eyes as he searched her slender frame for any signs of injury.

She looked grubby and tired but otherwise okay—the sight of him more distressing than whatever had happened to have her sending her sister a garbled text about being in a spot of trouble hours ago.

It looked like more than a spot to him.

He forced himself to take a deep breath.

*You've found her. She's okay. Now all you have to do is get her on a plane back to New York and you can forget about her again.*

The tension which had been grinding in the pit of his stomach since noon—and during the long hours of the afternoon, as he and a team of his men had combed the five square miles to where his IT guys had managed to triangulate her phone signal—began to ease. At least he'd found her before dark.

"I don't need rescuing," she said, her dazed expression hardening with animosity.

The fist which had been tightening around his throat for the last twenty minutes as he watched the sun head for the horizon thumped his larynx with a one-two punch.

"You're kidding, right?" His gaze drifted over

her, taking in the butt-hugging cut-offs, the dusty shirt, the tank top showing the subtle curve of her breasts, the filthy feet which… Where the heck were her shoes?

She planted one fist on her hip, the other one clinging to a carved wooden box that looked almost as heavy as she was. “No, I’m not kidding.”

She puffed with indignation, but the sweat-soaked hair stuck to her forehead stayed firmly in place. Unfortunately it did nothing to disguise her high cheekbones, the full, mobile mouth or the sunburnt patch on her nose. Or the exhaustion shadowing her mermaid-green eyes.

“I’m good,” she said, her arms tightening on the wooden box and her chin jutting out. “I don’t know how you found me, but you can just unfind me again. Okay?”

“No, that’s not okay.”

Frustration and extreme irritation twisted his insides.

It was a reaction he recognized. From the last time Dario had asked him to ride herd on his kid sister-in-law—and the single heartbeat of madness when he’d reacted without thinking to the sharp, spicy taste of that mouth.

“I’m not unfinding you,” he said. “And I’m not leaving you here. Dario wants you on a flight back to New York as soon as you’re found.”

Her eyebrows launched up her forehead. “I’m not going back to New York,” she said, sounding adamant for a woman who looked as if she was about to collapse. But then the box she was holding slipped. She struggled to regain it, stumbled, and then yelped as her bare foot landed on a rock.

"Okay, this conversation's over," he said.

Stepping forward, he scooped her and the box into his arms.

She gasped and went rigid. "Put me down." The angry glare infused the rest of her face with a shade of red to match her sunburn.

"Nope." The spicy scent of lemon, sea salt and female sweat tightened the screaming tension in his gut as he marched up the track toward his car.

"What do you mean no? I... *Oof!*"

He dumped her unceremoniously into the passenger seat and slammed the door. After striding around the front of the muscle car, he climbed into the driver's seat and turned on the ignition. "This isn't a negotiation."

Placing his arm across the back of her seat, he began to reverse down the track, wincing when he heard the muffler bounce off another rock.

"I see you still get off on ordering women about," she said, but the insult lacked heat.

He slipped his sunglasses on and ignored her. From their sparring matches five years ago, he knew her default position was mouthy and it was better not to engage.

Katherine Whittaker had always been a piece of work. But, if the tabloid press was to be believed, her behavior had gotten a whole lot worse in the years since her old man's trial and their aborted kiss in her housekeeper's Brooklyn apartment. She'd dropped off the radar for the past few months, but according to Dario that was only because she'd left Manhattan and had been bumming around Europe on her own, freaking her sister out. So, basically, Katherine Whittaker had just spent the last few months causing trouble incognito.

He backed onto the coast road, slotted the transmission into drive and hit the gas. He could feel her angry glare but didn't trust himself to speak.

This woman had everything—a lavish home, a family who loved her and the smarts to make something of herself. Instead of which, she'd chosen to thumb her nose at it all and behave like a kid in a candy store for years, probably all on Dario's dime.

"I don't know where you think you're taking me, but you can't *make* me do anything," she said.

He glanced across the console. Her tip-tilted eyes had gone squinty around the corners.

"I'm not nineteen years old anymore," she added. "And I don't take orders from anyone, least of all you."

He turned back to the road, but not before he'd noticed the rise and fall of her breasts beneath the soft cotton of her tank top.

"You want to get out and walk some more?" he asked, calling her bluff.

She glared at him but then swung her face away.

*I didn't think so.*

Her slim shoulders slumped against the seat—reminding him of the troubled nineteen-year-old with a big mouth and a crush on him he'd taken great pains to ignore, until she'd gotten under his guard for a few gut-wrenching seconds.

The dying sunlight caught the gold in her hair and made the sweat misting the slopes of her breasts glimmer. Reaction kicked him hard in the gut.

Sometime in the last five years, the gawky duckling with the smart and way too tempting mouth had turned into a long-legged and stunningly beautiful swan, even under the layer of dirt, sweat and animosity.

He punched the gas to pass a truck laden with fruit trees. The sooner he got rid of Katherine Whittaker, the better.

"Why are you even in Italy?" she murmured. "Please tell me you didn't come all this way just to get in my face?"

He let the snotty comment go, because even the hostile tone couldn't disguise the weary resignation.

"I'm staying on Capri until Monday," he said. "The company's running security for the press opening of the new Venus resort. Dario contacted me to coordinate the search when you texted Megan this morning."

"How fortuitous," she said, the bite of sarcasm dulled by fatigue.

Not that fortuitous, really. The Venus project was a major contract, but Jared hadn't planned to attend the event in person—despite all the noise from his PR department about the great publicity it would generate in the European market if he showed up for the four-day press launch. But his plans had changed this morning when Dario's call had come in from New York, interrupting him in Naples during a meeting where he'd been finalizing the takeover of a small tech-security firm.

The urgency in Dario's voice had hit first, then the wavc of shame at the mention of a girl he had tried very hard to forget in the last five years.

When he'd discovered that Katherine was missing on the Amalfi Coast somewhere, that her sister Megan was freaking out big time and that they hadn't been able to contract her, Jared hadn't hesitated.

He'd redirected a team of his men from the Venus project to kick-start the search, and then taken a helicopter to Sorrento.

He tapped his thumbs on the steering wheel. He still didn't know where that impulse had come from. Probably just his loyalty to Dario. It was true he'd never quite been able to forget Katherine Whittaker—and the desolation in her eyes after that aborted kiss—but he never got sentimental about women. Especially not women as troublesome as this one.

"How did you end up lost in Campania barefoot?" he asked, attempting to defuse the situation and get some answers. Although he suspected he already knew what had happened.

The Amalfi Coast was a mecca for billionaire property development and high-end tourism but, when you factored in the deprivation in Naples' slums less than thirty miles away, opportunistic robberies weren't uncommon.

"I'm not lost," she said, snapping his olive branch

in two. "I know where I am. And where I want to go. And it's not back to New York."

Yeah, it was. But he'd deal with the problem of getting her on a plane once they got to the airport. First he needed to swing by wherever she was staying so she could wash up and they could grab her luggage and travel documents.

Once she was on her way home, he'd follow up with the police on the investigation. Even if she hadn't been hurt, he wanted the little bastards who had done this to her caught and prosecuted.

"So, where were you headed with no transport and no shoes?"

"Sorrento. If you could drop me there, that would be terrific. Then you can tell Dario you've done your bit."

"Is that where you're based? In Sorrento?" he asked.

She cleared her throat. "Not exactly."

He glanced at her. The rosé blush was heading for her hairline at an alarming rate.

"Then where's the rest of your stuff?" he demanded.

"Probably half way to France by now on the back of my stolen Vespa, with my shoes."

Jared's fingers clenched on the wheel hard enough to leave an indent in the leather. "Please tell me that doesn't include your passport," he said.

The glare she sent him gave him the answer he didn't want.

# CHAPTER TWO

THE LAST OF the sunshine glinted off the convertible's paintwork as it powered down the winding coast road and cast shadows over Jared Caine's face, making him look even more forbidding than usual. The short, dark strands of his hair danced playfully in the breeze but did nothing to soften the line of his jaw—which he was clenching hard enough to crack a tooth.

His eyes were hidden behind the dark lenses of his designer sunglasses, but Katie didn't need to look into them to know Jared Caine was angry about the latest turn of events and trying hard not to show it.

*Join the club.*

She looked back toward the horizon and slipped down in the seat until the car's luxury leather upholstery cradled her. She closed her eyes, letting the well-oiled hum of the convertible's engine drown out the deep hum in her abdomen—which had kicked off the minute Caine had stepped out of his car—and was not remotely significant.

Caine was a phenomenally good-looking guy—

with a potent sexual charisma. Especially if you had a weakness for tough, take-charge, control-freaky types who demonstrated about as much empathy and sensitivity as the jagged rocks of Campania's coastline. And apparently she did, especially when she was exhausted and traumatized and had just been mugged.

Luckily, she had previous experience of this reaction. She would get over it.

And at least he'd stopped trying to bully her into getting on a plane. She might have been able to get some grim satisfaction out of thwarting his plan but for the painful throbbing in her frontal lobe as she tried to get her head around the huge mess she was in.

The car phone buzzed loudly, making her head hurt even more.

"Hey, Dario," Caine said, answering the call and then switching to speaker phone.

"Tell me you've found her, Jared?"

Katie's heart somersaulted in her chest at the urgency in her brother-in-law's voice and she straightened in her seat.

"I've got her here with me," Caine replied. "Picked her up on a farm track five miles from Sorrento. We're on speaker."

Dario cursed in Italian. "Katie? *Grazie Dio*," he murmured. "Are you okay? What happened?"

"I'm good, Dario. Really, it wasn't anything major. I got robbed, but they didn't hurt me. I didn't want you and Meg to worry."

"Is she okay, Jared?" Dario asked, even though she'd already answered that question.

Caine's all-seeing gaze swept over her, assessing her condition again, the way he had when he'd first stepped out of his car. And the hum went haywire.

She pressed her hand to her head, mindful of the graze hiding behind her hair which she didn't want either Caine or Dario to know about, because it would just give the two of them more excuses to treat her like a five-year-old.

"Other than sore feet, yes," he said after the disturbingly thorough examination. "Just shaken up."

"I'm sitting right here, Dario," she pointed out, trying not to lose her cool, while being reminded of being nineteen years old again and having both Dario and Caine decide that they knew what was best for her.

The spurt of indignation died though when she heard Megan's muffled voice and then her sister came on the line. "Katie, thank God you're okay. I've been worried sick ever since we got your text and I couldn't get through to you."

Guilt swept through Katie at the distressed tone.

"The phone lost service right after I texted you," Katie said, regretting sending the panicked plea in the moments after the robbery even more. Megan would have been frantic and it was all her fault, as usual. "Really, Megan, I'm fine," she repeated. "It's not a big deal."

"Where are you now?" her sister asked.

"With Caine, in his car."

*Hopefully heading for Sorrento.*

"We can wire you some money. How much do you need?" Megan cut back in.

Katie wanted desperately to refuse the offer, especially with Caine listening in. He'd once called her a spoiled brat and in her debilitated state the old insult felt fresh.

"Two hundred euros would be terrific," she said. It would be just enough to stay in a hostel for a couple of nights, contact her insurance company to replenish her wardrobe and get painting. Once she'd done a few watercolors she could set up a pitch in Piazza Tasso. Sorrento's main square was the perfect place for her to sell her work, with its arty vibe and the never-ending stream of tourists. "I'll pay you back as soon as I—"

"Don't be silly. That's not enough. Let us wire you five thousand." Megan interrupted her again, sounding desperate. "You need to pay for a plane ticket home."

"I'm not coming home, Meg," Katie said, trying not to sound defensive or, worse, ungrateful. But she knew she had to remain firm.

She wasn't ready to go back. Not yet.

"You're not?" Megan sounded devastated. "Even after this?"

"I'll be back soon. I promise," she said, mindful of their audience. She could feel Caine listening from across the car and judging.

Not to mention Dario, who she would bet was

scowling at the phone right now, not happy about the way she was upsetting his wife.

"You've been away for months now," Megan came back. "I can't bear for..." The line crackled and Katie's guilt began to choke her. Was Megan crying?

The hollow space in the pit of her belly got larger.

The muffled sounds finally silenced. Then a door shut and Dario's voice came over the phone. "Megan is resting now," he said, by way of explanation.

"Is she okay?" Katie asked, the guilt all but crippling her. She'd known Megan would worry, but she hadn't realized she'd worry this much. Megan was usually so practical and calm. "I'm so sorry to have caused—"

"Don't say that if it isn't true, *sorellina*," Dario cut in, using the endearment that had meant so much to Katie when he'd first started using it a few years ago.

*Little sister.*

"You say you are sorry for causing Megan this distress, but it is a simple matter to solve the problem." Her brother-in-law's usually flawless English had become disjointed, a sure sign he was holding on to his temper with an effort. "All you need to do is come home."

"I can't do that, Dario, please understand." Inadequacy twisted in her stomach, making unhappy bedfellows with the guilt.

*Why does this have to be so hard?*

She sounded immature and selfish, even to her own ears. But the thought of returning to New York had the inadequacy clawing at her throat, the way it had so often since the night of Whittaker's attack. She couldn't go back until she had more to show for her trip than some great anecdotes and a half-hearted show of independence.

The money she'd made over the last two months with her artwork was all gone, probably paying for a major Pinky and Perky party somewhere. The chances of getting it back were slim to none. She couldn't return to New York without it because she'd be right back where she started, with Dario and Megan bankrolling her and all her screw-ups.

She couldn't tell Dario and Megan about the money she'd lost, though, because they'd offer to replace it, not realizing that it wasn't the money that mattered so much as the fact she'd earned it herself.

"And when will you be ready?" Dario asked. "How much longer do you intend to punish your sister this way?"

"I'm not trying to punish Megan," she said, the weariness starting to weigh her down. Dario was someone she had always wanted to impress, because he had been the one to save Megan when she had failed. "This isn't about her. It's about me."

"Yes, I understand, it is always about you," Dario replied, the sharp tone unlike him. Dario rarely if ever showed his frustration.

"I'm sorry you feel that way," she said. "And I'm really sorry I contacted you with this. I shouldn't have done that, I should have—"

"No, Katie, don't say this. We are glad you contacted us," he said, but she could hear the weary sigh down the phone line—and felt like even more of a fraud.

Dario was always so certain. So successful. And so was Megan. They knew what they wanted and had set out to get it together. They'd had a few wobbles along the way. But they'd worked through them and succeeded and built an incredible life for themselves.

But what they had never understood was that she wasn't like them. She had none of Megan's steadiness or certainty and none of Dario's drive or ambition. And she simply wasn't cut out for long-term relationships. Heck, she'd never even gotten to third base with any of the guys she'd dated over the years—the fear of being subsumed, having her own personality swallowed up by someone else's, always so much greater than the lure of sexual intimacy.

That she was still a virgin at twenty-four years old spoke for itself. She didn't consider it a choice or a flaw, so much as an essential means of survival. She had to find herself first, really get to know who she was and what she wanted, before she could consider risking that fragile identity by blending it with another.

And, if she ever did find the right guy, it would never be a guy like Dario. As much as she loved him as a brother, marrying someone like him, falling in love with someone like him, would be an unmitigated disaster.

The way Megan and Dario looked at each other sometimes when they thought no one was watching, the way they touched each other—all those small, insignificant, secret touches that demonstrated not just their off-the-charts sexual chemistry but also how much they loved and respected each other—had always scared Katie. How could anyone trust another person that much? Enough to rely on them absolutely?

She couldn't do that—she knew she couldn't. But living so close to Megan and her family, watching Dario and Megan with their two adorable kids, Izzy and Arturo, had become a double-edged sword.

She loved being part of a solid, secure unit that wasn't just her and her sister anymore. But, on the other hand, seeing how happy, how complete, Megan, Dario and their kids were together made her feel like an intruder. The dark cloud on their bright horizon who could contribute nothing to the whole but could only take.

The tabloid stories of her dancing on tables, or getting arrested during a midnight swim in Central Park Lake, or losing her modeling contract because she had famously decided to chop all her hair off on a whim had hurt Megan and Dario and the kids as much as they'd hurt her.

Which was exactly why she'd jumped ship and headed to Europe where her celebrity profile was non-existent. The anonymity had been glorious. But, more than that, having to survive on her own had been liberating in ways she couldn't even have imagined.

She'd learned some important stuff about herself. Not least of which was that she could enjoy life, do adventurous, exciting stuff, without being reckless or stupid. Or dragging her family through the mud.

She'd discovered that after four and a half years of screw-ups and embarrassing tabloid headlines, after four and a half years of citations and fines as a result of a string of dumb stunts and thoughtless acts, and after four and a half years of failing to make anything like a decent living she could break that cycle. She could live on her own terms without compromising the happiness of others.

But New Improved Katie was still a work in progress. And today she was at a crossroads, her fledging independence being tested thanks to Pinky and Perky. But this time she couldn't take the easy road.

Getting Dario to understand why she didn't want his help was going to be an uphill battle, though. Not one she needed right now when she felt as if she were about to dissolve into Caine's upholstery.

"I am glad you contacted us," Dario reiterated. "But you must understand now that you are safer here, with your family, than wandering around Europe on your own," he continued, the no-nonsense tone one she was sure he used on his employees. "You must fly home tonight. And we will figure this out together."

*But it's not your problem, it's mine*, she wanted to scream. But the words were locked in her throat, trapped behind the boulder of guilt. How could she make Megan and him see that their love was stifling her ability to solve her own problems and not empowering her without hurting them even more?

"Dario, that's not going to happen, man," Caine's gruff voice sliced through Katie's anxiety. "She can't fly anywhere for a while."

Katie blinked, surprised not just by Caine's intervention but that he seemed to be on her side. A strange warmth spread through her to add to the inappropriate hum. Of course she didn't need his help, but she was exhausted enough to appreciate it, especially from someone who had always batted for Team Dario.

"Why not?" Dario asked, sounding frustrated.

"Because the muggers stole her passport."

The realization that Caine's defection was about pragmatism, rather than a newfound respect for her, dampened Katie's warm glow a little.

She shook off the prickle of disappointment. She didn't care what Caine's motives were, he'd just provided her with the perfect get-out clause—which if she hadn't been so exhausted she would have figured out herself.

"That's true, Dario," she chipped in. "I'm stuck here until I can get a new one." And replace everything else she'd lost, which would take her a month at least. Possibly more.

"Can you organize a new passport, Jared?" Dario said, as if she hadn't spoken.

"Sure."

"How long will it take?" Dario asked.

"Hey, wait a minute, I can…" Katie tried to interrupt but the men were already on a testosterone roll.

"I'll find out. I'll get my PA to contact the British consulate in Naples. My guess is, it'll be quicker than trying to get her a US one."

Katie's mind reeled. How did Jared Caine know she had dual nationality? She'd spent the years until her mother's death in a British boarding school, and her accent had always been a mid-Atlantic hybrid—her upbringing a mix of two cultures divided by a common language. But since her late teens she'd always thought of herself as more American than British, unlike Megan. How exactly was this any of Jared Caine's business, though?

"You are in Capri for the next few days, yes?" Dario asked.

"Yeah."

"Then she must stay with you, until the passport is ready. And you can bring her home? Is that okay?"

*What the...?*

Katie's tired mind stalled. For several precious seconds she was so shocked by Dario's high-handed assumption, no sound would come out of her mouth.

Caine paused, his jaw hardening to granite again. And Katie felt the horror and humiliation that had taken her by the throat begin to ease.

*Don't freak out. No way will Caine agree to this.*

Dario was being a jerk, but his heart was in the right place. Dario's I'm-the-boss-of-you gene had always been hyperactive, or he never would have whisked Meg off to Isadora after the assault and insisted on marrying her when he'd found out she was pregnant. And, if anything, since he had become a dad Dario's take-charge gene had gone into overdrive because there was nothing he wouldn't do to protect his children or his wife. And he'd always considered Katie part of that equation, even before he'd married Megan. Which was exactly how she'd ended up with Caine as a minder five years ago.

But Dario didn't know what had happened between her and his best friend while he and Megan had been in Isadora. She had certainly never told either Megan or him about that humiliating kiss. And she was sure Caine hadn't said anything to Dario, either, or Megan would have mentioned it.

The men were as close as brothers, but she'd never been able to get out of Megan what their history was. All she knew was that Caine seemed to owe Dario some kind of debt. But, whatever the debt was, it couldn't possibly be enough to make him agree to be her babysitter again.

"Of course it's not a problem." Caine's reply shocked Katie into silence again. "She can come to Capri with me until I fly back in four days—I'll make sure she has a passport by then."

"Great," Dario said. "That's settled."

"Are you completely mad?" Katie blurted out at the same time, finally relocating her voice.

"Katie?" Dario asked, obviously confused. "What is the matter?"

"I've got this, Dario. Gotta sign off—we're coming to a tunnel. Speak soon." Jared fired a glare at her as he disconnected the call with no tunnel in sight.

Adrenaline surged through her veins, her outrage

overtaking her exhaustion. "Why did you tell him that?" she yelped. "This is none of your business."

"It is now," he said, the bunched muscle in his jaw working overtime. He didn't look any happier at the prospect than she did.

She struggled to calm her breathing before her head exploded.

"This is ridiculous. I'm a grown woman," she said, attempting to appeal to his common sense before she gave herself an aneurysm. Fighting fire with fire didn't work with Caine. She'd tried that once before when she'd been a teenager and it had been a disaster. "Which means I decide what I do. Not you. Or Dario. And I have no intention of going to Capri, with or without you. So you need to call him back and tell him."

She'd rather gouge out her own eyeballs than go there during some huge PR event. Although the paparazzi and the press had probably forgotten all about her, she was not about to tempt fate. And going with Caine was out of the question. They didn't like each other and there was the inappropriate hum to consider.

And, on top of all that, Capri was the one place in Europe she had never wanted to go—because her mother was buried somewhere on that island, after the car she'd been in with one of her many lovers had plunged off a cliff. Katie had been to Capri once before, as an eight-year-old, and the hazy memory of standing over a grave in the misty rain, her sister's arm heavy on her shoulders and the caustic flash of camera bulbs blinding them both, was a blur of misery, emptiness and fear which she did not want to revisit.

The hollow pain in her stomach sunk into the floor of Caine's convertible.

This trip was about getting away from her mother's legacy—and the thoughtlessness Katie had inherited that could wreck lives if she didn't get a handle on it—not following in the woman's footsteps.

"I know you're a grown woman," he said, the growled acknowledgment setting off a new hum that made no sense at all, so she ignored it. "But you're a grown woman with no money, no clothes, no means of transportation and no ID, which means you're all out of options. You can't even collect the money Megan's planning to wire you."

Tears of frustration stung the back of her eyes at his brutal assessment, the unfairness of the situation making her want to weep.

"Then lend me some money. I'll pay you back, I swear." She could hear the pathetic plea in her voice and hated herself for it. But what other choice did she have? He was right. She couldn't survive with nothing. But why should everything she'd worked so hard to achieve in the last few months be ruined simply because she'd had the misfortune to get mugged?

"Admit it, you don't want to babysit me anymore than I want to be babysat," she continued. "If you could give me enough to sort myself out for a few days, I can contact Dario and explain everything. There's no reason for you to even be involved."

He didn't say anything, his jaw still rigid. She thought she might have made progress. But, when he glanced her way, his gaze locked on her forehead and he swore.

She gripped the dash as the car swerved to the side of the road and stopped.

Her back thudded against the car door and she brushed the hair that had been lifted by the breeze back over her forehead. But when he took her elbow and tugged her toward him, she knew it was too late.

"Hold still," he said. He brushed a fingertip over her forehead to lift her hair out the way, and studied the bruise for what felt like several hours.

Temper and something inscrutable swirled in the deep-blue depths before he held up three fingers. "How many?"

"Three."

Folding two down, he tracked his index finger past her nose and back again. "Follow it."

She did as she was told as her heart pummeled her ribs, and the stupid hum in the pit of her abdomen spiked. The intense look was one she remembered.

"Did you pass out when it happened?" he asked, his expression set in grim lines.

"No."

"Are you sure?"

"I'm not an idiot," she managed round the clump of cotton wool that seemed to be clogging her tonsils. "If I thought I had a concussion, I would have said something."

One eyebrow cocked. "You should have said

something, period. If you didn't look so done in right now, I would be forced to revise my rule on spanking women."

To her horror, even in the depths of her exhaustion a flare of heat crossed her buttocks. She stiffened and tugged her elbow out of his grasp.

What was wrong with her? How could she get some weird, prurient thrill out of being threatened with a spanking like an unruly kid?

"Then I guess I'd be forced to revise my rule on chopping off men's arms," she managed at last. But the comeback wasn't one of her best, as hopelessness began to engulf her. Not only was she at Caine's mercy, for tonight at least, she also appeared to be at the mercy of the wayward libido she thought she'd tamed five years ago.

She clasped her arms around her waist, rubbing the goose bumps which had risen on her flesh despite the warm evening air.

He took a bottle of water out of the glove box and dampened a wad of tissues. Tucking a finger under her chin, he lifted her face to hold the cold compress to the bump on her forehead.

Grasping her wrist, he lifted her hand to replace his. "Keep it pressed to the wound," he said. The shuttered look he sent her made the churning in her stomach worse. Being pitied was hardly an improvement on being patronized.

"My launch is docked at the Marina Grande," he said, mentioning Sorrento's main port. "I'll call ahead and get a doctor to meet us there, so they can check out your head before we leave Sorrento."

"That's overkill. It's only a graze." And she hadn't actually agreed to go to Capri with him. But the thought of having that argument again felt overwhelming—seeing as she could hardly string a coherent sentence together.

He sent her a quelling look and she knew she wasn't going to win this argument either. "How did it happen?" he asked.

"The battle for my pack got a little out of hand."

Temper flashed in his eyes, disconcerting her, because it didn't appear to be aimed at her. For once. "How many of them were there?"

"Two, but they were just teenagers. I don't think they meant to hurt me."

"So what? They did," he said. "I want a description. I'll file a report with the local cops and brief my team on Capri. Those little bastards need to be caught and punished."

There he went, assuming she was going to Capri with him again… But her objections remained locked in her throat, beaten into submission by the low fury in his tone and the news he was going to get his men to help find her muggers. The wobbly sensation it caused in her tummy had to be exhaustion.

She didn't want an avenging angel any more than she wanted a white knight. And especially not one like Jared Caine whose control-freak tendencies were only slightly less disturbing than his ability to make her insides vibrate as if she were plugged into an electric socket.

He shifted into gear and pulled back onto the road. The sun was setting, adding a vivid glow to the stunning landscape as they approached Sorrento. Colorful terracotta houses perched precariously over the vivid blue of the Mediterranean, punctuated by orange groves and trellises of grape vines. A train decorated with colorful graffiti rattled past on the hillside above them.

After calling his PA to arrange a doctor to meet them at the port, and coaxing a surprisingly detailed description of Pinky and Perky out of Katie, Caine contacted the local police force on speaker phone to report the crime. She let her mind drift as she listened to him talk to the dispatcher in Italian, the lyrical language making his deep voice sound even more compelling. She'd only been in Italy a month, and her Italian was still patchy, but his accent sounded perfect. Why was she not surprised? Was there nothing the man didn't excel at?

The dying sunlight cast the angles of Caine's face into sharp relief. No wonder she'd had such a crush on him as a nineteen-year-old—the man was scarily gorgeous with a confidence most women would find irresistible. But not her, she told herself, determined to believe it.

He finished the call as they entered the city's narrow streets, and she forced herself to make one last-ditch attempt to salvage her pride and self-respect, not to mention her sanity. Because four days on Capri with him was liable to threaten all three.

"Are you sure you don't want to just lend me some money and let me stay here?" she asked. "I really don't need a keeper. Whatever Dario thinks."

He took his sunglasses off as the twilight descended and sent her a level look. "Not gonna happen, so give it up," he said with a determination that dashed her last hope. "And, just for the record, Dario's not the only one who thinks you need a keeper."

She huffed out a breath. She should have been upset by the high-handed comment. But she was now officially too tired and too miserable to care. Her head was throbbing, her feet hurt and her nose was beginning to sting from what felt like third-degree sunburn. And then there was the blasted hum to consider, which was making her giddy.

"Has anyone ever told you you're a bully?" she muttered.

"Frequently," he said, then a strange thing happened. The sensual line of his lips lifted on one side drawing her attention to the scar on his top lip. She might have missed the movement, because it was there one second and gone the next. But even that tiny flicker—the infinitesimal crack in the controlled facade—had a devastating effect on her equilibrium as the hum plunged.

Her face heated, the atmosphere suddenly too close, too intimate, despite the salty breeze as they took the road down to Marina Grande.

Lights glittered on the cliff top as Sorrento woke up for the night, the Palladian splendor of the Hotel Excelsior Vittoria beaming down on the harbor like a reigning queen. But the view wasn't anywhere near as breathtaking as the barest hint of a smile on Jared Caine's lips.

Had she ever seen him smile before? She couldn't have. Because that crooked half-smile—rare and rusty—was a secret weapon in the man's arsenal she had been unaware of. As if he didn't already have enough weapons at his disposable.

"Just so you know, I make a terrible house guest," she added, not happy that he'd managed to get the upper hand so easily. "I always leave the top off the toothpaste and I never put anything away. You're going to hate having me there."

"Our villa has two bathrooms," he replied as he took a left past the main port at the bottom of the cliff road. "And staff to clean up after you. I'll manage."

Our *villa?* So they were going to be sharing a villa.

The hum became a deep primal buzz.

They drove past the concrete dock where passengers were boarding the evening ferry to Ischia. He slowed the car to a crawl to inch past a couple of waterfront restaurants already filled with tourists watching the last of the sunset. The pungent scent of raw fish and garlic wafted past as they approached rows of fishing boats, leisure dinghies and small yachts bobbing on the water. The car edged to a stop at the very end of the waterfront where a private dock protruded out into the bay. A huge motor launch stood at the end of the floating wooden platform, the stainless-steel stanchions gleaming red in the fading sunlight.

He braked and got out of the car. Reaching into the back, he lifted out her art box and hefted it under his arm. The sunset shone on his onyx hair as he came round to open her door. "How are the feet?" he asked. "Do you need me to carry you on board?"

"No. My feet are fine." *Give or take a million and one blisters.*

She stepped out of the car, struggling not to flinch as her tortured soles connected with the worn wood of the dock. But she'd rather walk across hot coals than give him another excuse to scoop her up again. Being in such close proximity to that broad, heavily muscled chest and his disconcertingly delicious scent would increase the disturbing buzz.

She took her time making her way toward the boat, far too aware of his powerful presence beside her, waiting to step in again if she stumbled. She couldn't help the sigh of relief, though, when she was able to lean on the guardrail of the gangplank.

A young man, wearing a peaked cap greeted them on deck and took her art box from Jared, after introducing himself as Matteo, the launch's pilot. He had a brief conversation with Jared. From her smattering of Italian, she gathered Dr. Chialini would be arriving shortly, but was based in Sorrento so couldn't travel with them to Capri.

Jared seemed to want to argue the point.

"It's okay. I really don't need a doctor anyway," she interrupted in English. But as both men swung toward her she made the mistake of letting go of the guardrail.

The boat swayed slightly and her knees gave way as blood rushed to her aching head with startling speed.

Hard hands grasped her upper arms, catching her before she could hit the deck.

A rough, urgent curse beckoned her back from toppling into the abyss.

She locked her knees as Caine's fingers pressed into her biceps.

"Why didn't you say you were feeling faint?"

"I'm just tired," she said, but the earthquake which had started in her legs was still sending aftershocks through her body.

"You're shaking," he said, his tone raw. The rough calluses on his palm sent ripples of sensation sizzling across her skin. Then suddenly she was weightless.

Her breath got trapped in her lungs as she ingested a lungful of his scent, the subtle hint of salt, soap and man. She was too close to him.

Close enough to detect the scar again which had once fascinated her through the shadow of stubble. Close enough to see the silver shards in the cool blue of his irises.

Her heartbeat slammed into her throat.

"What are you doing?" she asked, her voice sounding far away. "I told you, I can walk."

He glanced at her, the muscle in his cheek flexing. “Shut up, Katherine.”

She wanted to insist he put her down, but she couldn’t find the strength to do anything, her limbs so numb she felt as if they weren’t her own. He crossed the deck in a few strides, then took the steps down into a cabin with her held securely in his arms. The flex of his biceps felt hard against her back, the wall of his chest solid against her cheek. Her pulse jumped and jived.

The luxury interior was furnished with deep leather couches built into the hull. Large portholes afforded a view of the edge of the dock and the sea beyond, the full moon lifting over the horizon as the last of the sun fled.

Caine deposited her on the couch. “Do you feel nauseous?”

“No, I’m okay, really.”

Before they could argue the point, the good Dr. Chialini appeared. Caine hovered throughout the examination, firing off questions to the doctor in Italian as the poor woman tried to do her job. Katie held her tongue and did as she was told. If he got his caveman act out of his system, maybe he’d back off.

After declaring Katie concussion-free, and giving her a dose of painkillers for her headache, the doctor cleaned Katie’s feet. She found only a few small cuts and abrasions, which she dabbed with antiseptic cream and covered with plasters.

“Keep the cuts clean, and wear soft shoes or go barefoot if they are too sore,” she said in her perfect English as she packed her black case.

*Not a problem*, Katie thought wryly, *seeing as I don't actually have any shoes*.

Caine continued to quiz the doctor as he left the cabin with her. Katie could hear them talking as they went up on deck together but was way too tired to decipher what was being said.

She stretched out on the couch, watching the lights on the headland as the voices drifted into silence, followed by the rumble of the boat's engine.

*Next stop, Capri. The site of one of my worst memories. And four days spent in Jared Caine's overwhelming company.*

She listened to the waves slapping against the hull, felt the kick of movement as the boat peeled away from the dock, and breathed in the scene of new leather and sea air.

Caine would probably be back in a minute to micromanage her. She closed her eyes. Well, he couldn't bully her if she was comatose.

The salty breeze coming from the deck ruffled the short hairs on her arms as her limbs became weightless. She floated, buoyed by the bone-deep fatigue which had been lurking at the edges of her consciousness for hours. But as the gentle sway of the boat lulled her into a deep, drugging sleep, the buzz refused to fade.

"I'll need some clothes," Jared spoke into his cell phone as he stood in the entrance to the cabin and watched Katherine sleep.

She'd curled up on the couch like a child, her

hands under one cheek, her bare feet tucked under her butt.

"Do you know what size your guest is, Mr. Caine?"

Jared frowned, his gaze absorbing the long, coltish line of her body, the gentle rise and fall of her breasts beneath the grubby tank top. "No. Bring a selection."

"We could hire a stylist—arrange for them to come to your villa tomorrow morning and fit her for a new wardrobe," the resort concierge suggested helpfully.

"Great. Whatever," he said, not wanting to think about her slim frame and how it had felt so fragile in his arms.

"Will she be attending events with you?" the concierge asked.

He considered the question for a moment. "What events, exactly?"

He hated PR junkets. The original plan had been to fly in from Naples at the end of the weekend for one night and then head back to New York. But because of the woman curled up in front of him—who didn't look like she had a care in the world—he was going to be stuck on Capri for four days at least. Possibly more, if it took longer to get her a replacement passport.

"We have the investors' ball tomorrow," the concierge began. "Then the press picnic on Saturday afternoon and the gala on Sunday. There are a number of other events that the resort would love you to attend too, if you're not too busy with the security teams."

The truth was the security teams didn't need his oversight, but he planned to give it to them anyway, so he could spend as little time as possible going stir-crazy in a luxury villa he was being forced to share with his house guest.

The trickle of unease worked its way down his spine at the thought of having to share a villa with anyone. After living on the street—his crib being anything from a hotly contested doorway on the Upper West Side to a patch of turf in Harlem over a subway grate—his creature comforts were important to him, and he insisted on complete privacy.

He didn't share bed space or any other space. Especially not overnight.

He swallowed past the ripple of anxiety. And the pulse of heat.

He wasn't going to be sharing a bed with Katherine, just a villa. Luckily he'd booked a two-bed, because there'd been no other availability. But she would be in another room. And would no doubt want to avail herself of the resort's spa and leisure activities. Plus, the soundproofing in his room would be sufficient if… His jaw tensed. He wasn't going to have any episodes. He hadn't had any in months.

Even so, frustration twisted in his gut to tangle with the unwelcome swell of heat.

He should have said no to Dario's request. He didn't like the volatility of his attraction to this woman, especially as it made no sense. But he could never say no to Dario, because he owed the guy everything.

Katie mumbled in her sleep as the boat hit a swell.

"Signore Caine, do you want me to list the other events we have scheduled?" the concierge prompted on the other end of the line.

"Put me down for the ball," he said. If he was going to be here, he might as well make a couple of appearances. "Otherwise, make my excuses."

"Will Ms. Whittaker be attending with you?" the concierge asked.

He frowned, suppressing his kneejerk desire to say no.

The less time he spent with Katherine, the easier it would be for them both. But, as he watched her sleeping, it occurred to him that sometimes the easy option wasn't the smart option.

Perhaps he should rope her into the circus too. Given her aptitude for PR stunts, she'd enjoy the press attention—and it might stop her from getting up to mischief. He didn't trust her not to run off if left too much to her own devices.

Whatever happened, he was delivering her to Dario in New York as promised. And entertaining her in public was a lot less dangerous than entertaining her in private.

"Yeah, Ms. Whittaker will attend the ball with me."

"Wonderful, Signore Caine, I'll add you both to the guest lists."

Ending his call with the concierge, he headed back on deck.

But, as he let the sea spray mist his face, it didn't do a lot to cool the heat flowing through his veins.

He would have been quite happy never to see Katherine Whittaker again in this lifetime. And now he was going to be stuck with her for several days. He didn't like it one bit.

But what choice did he have? As soon as Dario had asked, he'd been bound to say yes. Hell, he'd pretty much do anything for that guy. But right this second, with his groin throbbing like a sore tooth, he couldn't help thinking that committing murder would be easier than spending four days sharing a two-bedroom villa with Katherine Whittaker.

He gripped the guard rail, absorbing the punch and roll of the boat's wake as Matteo heeled to starboard to steer past the point and head toward the Venus Resort's private dock on the far side of the island.

He took a moment to get his volatile reaction to her under control and the awareness which had arched between them the minute he'd laid eyes on her again—as if it had been five minutes since they'd last seen each other, not five years.

Katie braced her feet on the motor launch as it approached Capri, so tired now she felt as if she were drifting through a heavy fog. Caine had woken her up ten minutes ago, given her a pair of oversize socks to cover her feet which he'd borrowed from Matteo then spoken to her in low tones about the plans for the next few days. Not that she'd heard a word he was saying—his deep, hum-inducing voice was disturbing enough.

She searched the coastline, the rocky cliffs gilded by the full moon.

Her mother was buried somewhere on this island. But she felt strangely ambivalent about it, because all she could focus on at the moment was the overpowering presence of the man beside her.

Moonlight cast a pale, shimmering light onto the water as the pilot edged the launch into the resort's private dock. Katie dropped her head back to take in the luxury villas adding pale speckles to the greenery above them.

A bird of prey hovered above the bay as the launch slotted expertly into its berth, and then the hunting bird's dark silhouette swooped down and disappeared into the water as it captured some unsuspecting fish. Katie's stomach swooped with it as Caine stepped closer, his dark hair given an unearthly glow in the bright moonlight.

"You okay to walk?" he said, his deep voice radiating skepticism.

"Yes," she said, her soles now as numb as the rest of her in the soft woolen socks.

"You sure about that?" he asked.

"Positive," she said, and braced herself for an argument. But to her surprise it didn't come.

She stepped down the gangplank gingerly and onto the dock, ignoring her juddering pulse and rubbery legs.

Matteo was already tying off the boat's line.

He tipped his cap at her. Jared had a brief conversation with him in Italian before the young man disappeared up the gangplank.

"Oh, I forgot my stuff," she said. "I should go..."

Jared halted her attempts to return to the boat by putting a large hand firmly on her arm. "What's in it? Do you need it tonight?"

"No, I...I—" She stuttered to a halt. Mentioning the contents seemed strangely intimate, as if she would be telling him a secret about herself. "It's my art equipment. Paints, charcoal, that sort of thing."

"I'll make sure the staff bring it up to our villa tomorrow."

*Our* villa? Her mind snagged on the single syllable again and she forgot about the art box. The trapped feeling made her breath lurch in her lungs.

"Let's go," he said. "As soon as we get there, you can wash up and then crash out."

The thought of a shower was welcome, until his large palm settled on her spine to direct her down the dock. Warm pressure sizzled through the thin cotton and she stiffened, the trapped feeling intensifying the rush of heat.

A monstrous black motorcycle stood on the dock, the silver logo catching the light from the moon. Once they reached it, Caine lifted the only helmet off the handlebars, fitted it over her head then fastened the strap.

He swung his leg over the huge machine, kicked it off its stand then glanced over his shoulder. "Climb aboard."

She contemplated the bike.

*Just get on. He's not bothered—why should you be?*

But she *was* bothered as she placed trembling fingers on his shoulders and felt the muscles tense. Finding a foothold above the gleaming silver exhaust pipe, she breathed through her mouth and clambered onto the machine.

The two-tiered seat forced her legs wide, positioning her bottom so that her knees gripped his waist. The seam of her shorts rubbed the aching spot between her legs as she tried to push her sock-covered feet down and ease away from him. The salty air tinged with the musk of pine soap filled her lungs. Standing on the ignition pedal, he kicked down and the engine roared to life, the powerful purr sending sensation shimmering up through her buttocks.

His wrist twisted to adjust the throttle and the engine roared louder.

"You're gonna have to hold on tighter," he shouted over his shoulder. "I don't want you falling off on the ride up."

Forced to agree, she edged along the seat and leaned into him. She pressed her face into the solid muscles of his spine and spread her legs even wider to reach far enough around him to flatten her hands on his abdomen. Washboard abs rippled like velvet-covered steel.

The bare skin of her inner thighs absorbed the subtle rasp of his suit pants.

The bike lurched forward and she tightened her

grip reflexively. Tension rippled through his abs. Her breath shuddered out then jerked in again, filling her tortured lungs with a heady burst of his scent—the combination of soap and musk now mixed with the intoxicating scent of motor oil.

Every single one of her pulse points throbbed in unison as he weaved the motorbike down the deserted dock and then hit the single-track tarmac road etched into the cliff face.

The dock dropped away as they climbed the switchbacks at a steady speed. She noticed the canopy of stars above their heads, remarkably clear and bright in the night sky. And, despite her mind screaming at her not to, her body couldn't seem to stop itself from relaxing into the hard line of his.

Cocooned against him, she absorbed the strength of his muscled back. He felt so sure and solid and unyielding, as if he were a Roman god and she were being kidnapped on the back of his winged horse.

Reaching the top of the cliff, the bike rumbled along a secluded path, fragrant with the heady scent of bougainvillea. The ethereal white of a Romanesque villa appeared.

Katie tried to deepen her breathing and focus on the horizon and the cluster of lights along the Sorrentine coastline in the distance—rather than the waves of hair brushing the back of Caine's shirt collar, the subtle flex of his abdominal muscles beneath her palms or that delicious scent.

But her breathing remained choppy and shallow—because it wasn't the serene beauty of the Tyrrhenian sea, the craggy magnificence of Capri's limestone coves or even the hazy bulk of the peninsula in the distance that was making her light-headed.

It was the bossy, enigmatic and overwhelming man she was currently clinging on to.

# CHAPTER THREE

KATIE AWOKE THE next morning in a tangle of bedclothes—her body still throbbing from a kaleidoscope of erotic dreams driven by the feel of Jared's abs, warm and resilient beneath her fingertips, the scent of his hair in the breeze, the dropping sensation in her stomach as they'd climbed the switchbacks in the darkness.

She blinked at the sun shining through open doors on the far side of the luxurious room, bringing with it the aroma of honeysuckle and sea air.

The room was dominated by a four-poster draped with swathes of white linen. She vaguely remembered collapsing into the bed the night before, after sleepwalking through a shower in the lavishly tiled bathroom.

She spied a breakfast tray on a wrought-iron table on the balcony laden with exotic fruit and delicate pastries, steam rising from a pot of fresh coffee.

Her stomach growled in protest. Ignoring the subtle ache in her limbs and the sting in her feet, she hauled herself out of bed. Unable to find the dusty clothes she had folded on top of the dresser the night before, she dragged on the bathrobe she remembered discarding after last night's shower.

She would have to face Caine eventually, but first she needed sustenance. And clothing.

Tearing off a corner of a flaky croissant, she took in the view from the room's private balcony. A sparkling infinity pool nestled into a grove of lemon trees dominated the terraced gardens below. Trellised walkways covered with wisteria and bougainvillea vines bisected lawns edged with palm trees and wildflowers. The estate's panoramic aspect was stunning, the vista of towering cliffs—the limestone crags accented with bursts of wildflowers and shrubs—perfectly juxtaposed with the deep, iridescent blue of the sea. Katie poured herself a cup of coffee and loaded it with cream and sugar, itching to capture the scene in watercolor. Or maybe gouache. How else could she do justice to all the textures and tones? The bright, vivid colors?

She tucked into her breakfast, contemplating the play of light, and wondering if she could simply hide away in the villa's gardens and paint until her passport arrived.

But as the sun rose overhead, she let go of the dream. She would have to speak to Caine first, find her clothing and also contact her insurance company. Painting in the nude probably wasn't a good idea, given the disturbing dreams that had kept her tossing and turning during the night.

A knock sounded on the bedroom door and her heart jumped into her throat.

"Come in," she said, yanking the robe closed.

A maid appeared, and Katie's heart settled back into her chest.

"Signorina Whittaker, you are finished with your breakfast?"

"Yes, thank you." Katie forced a smile as the young woman walked onto the balcony. "Is Mr. Caine here?"

The woman smiled back as she cleared the breakfast dishes. "Signor Caine, he is at the resort." Before Katie could assess the odd combination of relief and disappointment at the news, the maid added, "But the *styllista*, she waits for you."

*Styllista?* "I'm sorry, I don't know what that means."

The maid nodded enthusiastically and gestured to the robe. "She is for your *nuovi vestiti* and *pantaloni.*"

New dresses and pants? Was she talking about a stylist? But she couldn't afford a stylist. Or new clothes, yet.

"But I haven't spoken to my insurance company?" Katie said to no one in particular because the maid simply ushered her off the balcony and toward the door of the suite.

"She waits, yes, you must go," the girl said.

Grasping the robe tightly around her neck, Katie forced herself to leave the sanctuary of the bedroom.

The villa's communal living area had been

shrouded in darkness the night before as Katie had made her excuses to Caine and rushed to her room. Now flooded with midmorning light, the airy open-plan room made much more of an impression. As lavish but as simply furnished as the bedroom, a stylish seating area of dark leather couches surrounded a cavernous fireplace filled with a vase of fresh flowers. Marble floors led out onto a terrace framed by archways fashioned in white stucco. At one end of the terrace stood a large area obviously made for *al fresco* dining, the canopy draped in white linen which fluttered in the sea breeze.

Three women stood in the center of it, surrounded by rails of clothing and fabrics draped over the chairs and tables. It looked like an explosion in a designer boutique.

Before Katie could figure out what this all meant, one of the women spotted her and dashed over to greet her.

"At last, Signorina Whittaker, you are awake." The compact and stylishly dressed middle-aged woman made Katie feel even more self-conscious about the lack of clothing she had on under her bathrobe. Taking her firmly by the arm, the woman led her onto the terrace and toward her two companions, talking a mile a minute in heavily accented but perfect English. "We have much to do and only a short time. For tonight's ball, I have a selection of ready-to-wear from the shops in Ana Capri to chose from, as we do not have time to get a gown made. I think your coloring would work best with..."

*Tonight's ball? What the...?*

Katie stumbled to a halt in front of the plethora of clothes. "I'm sorry, I don't know who you are. Or what you're talking about?"

Her head literally spun, the array of colors and textures hurting her eyes.

"I am Donatella Regiano." The woman pasted on an enthusiastic smile. "Signore Caine has hired me as your stylist. To arrange your new wardrobe, while you are on the island." Her gaze took on an eager glint as it roamed over Katie. "You are very slender. I have several gowns that will look *bellisima*."

She grasped Katie's hand and lifted it for examination. "But we have much to do to prepare for tonight, yes?" She spread her hand toward the two other women who hovered nearby, smiling with equal enthusiasm. "This is Marcella, who will handle your skin care and beauty needs," the stylist said, indicating a young woman about Katie's age armed with a large beautician's case. "And this is Sophia, the island's top hairstylist," she continued. The other woman, whose expertly coiled hair draped down her back in corkscrew curls, bowed in greeting, making the brushes and combs in the tool-belt she wore clatter together.

Katie snatched her hand back, feeling overwhelmed. She hadn't had a manicure in close to six months and had been hacking off her own hair when necessary since she'd left the US. So Caine had sicced the beauty police on her. The hollow stab of inadequacy was followed by a wave of panic.

She needed clothes, and she could see among the garments laid out an array of everyday wear—albeit designer stuff she doubted she could afford—but what ball was Donatella talking about? Was she supposed to be going to one…with Caine? She tried to recall the conversation they'd had in the launch's cabin when he'd woken her from her sleep during the ride over. Had he mentioned this? Had she agreed to something she couldn't remember while groggy and half-asleep?

"This hair is good." Donatella plunged her fingers into the unruly blond fuzz on Katie's head. She reeled off a barrage of instructions to Sophia in Italian. Katie started to feel under siege.

"Do not be concerned, we will not lose that wild quality," Donatella added.

More Italian instructions were fired at the hairdresser, who nodded sagely.

"It is very attractive," Donatella continued. Katie pressed her hands to her head to control the unruly locks, self-consciousness making her breakfast turn over in her belly. She'd always been a tomboy growing up and had never felt comfortable with this kind of attention. It was one of the reasons she'd never settled into a career as a model, the hours of makeup and styling always having left her feeling like an impostor in her own skin.

"It makes a statement, I think." Donatella's smile became mischievous. "That you will be as wild and willful in bed, tempting any man to tame you. Especially a man such as Signor Caine, no?" the woman added with a confidential wink as if they shared a naughty secret.

Realization hit.

Donatella thought she and Caine were lovers, that she was his mistress. Hot color scorched her chest and rose up her neck to fire across her cheeks.

Had Caine said as much to these women? Why on earth would he do that?

But the indignation she wanted to feel was incinerated as the erotic dreams which had tortured her during the night slammed into her.

Her thighs trembling with the powerful purr of the motorbike's engine, her sex yearning for Caine's expert touch. Her fingertips burning to explore the ridged strength of Caine's abdominal muscles. Her tongue thirsting to lick the tanned skin of his nape and kiss the sensitive hollow beneath his ear lobe.

"*Signor Caine è molto sexy, si*?" Marcella sent her a congratulatory smile, obviously misunderstanding the color now running riot over her face.

Panic and mortification consumed her at her visceral reaction to him now and all through the night. She tightened the belt on the robe and struggled to control the inferno blazing inside her.

"What is wrong, Signorina Whittaker?" Donatella had stopped smiling.

"Nothing, I just..." She paused, humiliated beyond belief. "I need to speak to Mr. Caine." She glanced at the exquisite designer items Donatella had laid out for her consideration, searching for a plausible excuse to call a halt to the styling session.

"I can't afford to buy anything until I've spoken to my insurance company." And she doubted what they would give her would cover stuff this expensive.

Donatella's face softened, her puzzled expression becoming smug. "Do not worry about this. Signor Caine is paying for everything."

*What?*

Katie almost choked on the thought. Why would he do that? Unless…?

"That's very nice of him," she said, humiliation and panic giving way to indignation. Was he buying her clothing to put her even more in his debt and under his control? "But I really can't accept it."

Donatella frowned, obviously confused by Katie's reply. "But I have something perfect for tonight, a bronze silk that will look stunning with your hair."

The woman continued to prattle on about different styles that would flatter her figure, sifting through the evening gowns and cocktails dresses, the pants and blouses. She displayed shoes in every conceivable color and style, then opened a large box filled with enough lingerie to sink a battleship. The sight of the delicate lace and silk items had the heat firing across Katie's cheeks again.

"I'm so sorry, but I can't take it. Any of it."

Donatella's smile became astute as she pulled a folded piece of paper out of a pocket in the linen suit she wore and handed it to Katie. "Signor Caine has left you a note, to tell you of his wishes."

*His wishes?*

Katie grabbed the sheet of paper and read the thick black scrawl.

*Get what you need. It's on me. The event's at eight. I'll be back by then to escort you.*
*Caine*

Katie screwed the note up in her fist and shoved it into the pocket of her robe. Her stomach twisted into tight, greasy knots as she imagined the independence she'd worked so hard for being eroded by Caine's arrogant dictate.

"This is good, no? You can have whatever you desire. And Signore Caine will pay." Donatella sent Katie a mercenary smile and Katie paled. She had to get out of this.

As the woman selected a gown from the rail to measure against Katie's frame, Marcella and Sophia headed off to set up a makeshift beauty parlor in Katie's lavish *en suite* bathroom.

The deep rumble of the motorbike outside cut the breeze.

*Caine.*

Excusing herself, Katie rushed through the living area, her bare feet slapping against the cool marble, propelled by panic and indignation. She stepped into the carport, sheltered by vines and trellises, just as Caine shoved the bike onto its stand.

Her heart crashed into her throat. She'd never seen him in casual clothes before and the effect was devastating, the illusion of sophistication supplied by his work wear gone.

Denim faded at the stress points hugged his muscular thighs while plain black cotton molded the solid bulge of his pecs and the ridges of his abdominal muscles. His hair stuck up in sweaty tufts as he pulled off the helmet and clipped it to the bike's handlebars. He ran his fingers through the thick, dark waves, tugging them into rows.

All the moisture dried up in her mouth as the erotic dreams came back full force. He lifted off his sunglasses and tucked them into the pocket of his jeans.

Pure blue eyes locked on her face—his all-seeing gaze drifting down her torso and setting off a tidal wave of reaction.

Her nipples squeezed into aching peaks and the hot spot between her thighs throbbed. The fluffy white toweling suddenly felt completely see-through.

One dark brow hiked up and the hint of a smile tugged at his sensual lips. "Hello, Katherine. I see Ms. Regiano and her crew haven't arrived yet."

The disorientating blast of heat she couldn't control swept through her and she forced her fury to the fore to mask her fear. How could he have this effect on her when no other man ever had? She didn't want to be like her mother, driven by urges beyond her control.

"She's here," she said, the blockage in her throat shattering. "But I can't afford those clothes."

His brows lowered. "I'm paying—didn't she give you my note?"

"You're not paying for my clothes. I can pay for my own clothes once I've contacted the insurance company." She wrapped her arms tightly around her waist, far too aware of her nakedness. And the gaze focused on her with the intensity of a hungry wolf. "Why did you tell her I was your mistress?"

He leaned back against the bike, crossing his legs at the ankles and folding his arms across his chest. The action made the muscles in his shoulders bunch as he studied her.

"I didn't," he said. "I haven't met her—the concierge hired her."

The direct reply gave her pause, but only for a moment. "Then why does she think we're lovers?" she cried.

The nonchalant shrug made it abundantly clear he didn't consider her pride and self-respect of any consequence. "Perhaps because you're living with me and wandering around the villa in a bathrobe?"

"I don't have a choice," she said, the injustice of the situation only adding to her anxiety. How could he remain so calm and pragmatic, so controlled, when her insides were turning to mush? "I don't know where my clothes are. Do you?"

"I told the staff to get rid of them."

"What?" she gasped, astounded by his arrogance.

"They were filthy. Seemed easier to just buy you more," he said, as if spending a fortune on a new wardrobe for her was no big deal.

"But they were my only clothes, until I can claim on my insurance or they find my pack."

"They have found your pack," he said. "That's why I came back, to let you know."

"Really?" She clung to the news. Was it possible that a little of this nightmare was over? There would be no money left, but if she at least had the rest of her belongings she wouldn't be so powerless, so reliant on his charity. "Did they find my passport?"

"No," he said, dashing the vain hope. "Everything of value was gone, and the clothes had to be destroyed, because those little bastards dumped the lot in a field full of starving goats."

"I see." Katie bit in to her bottom lip to stop it quivering, the flicker of pity in Caine's dispassionate gaze and the persistent hum only adding to her misery.

*Well, that's me totally screwed, then.*

Jared clamped down on the dumb urge to comfort her. She looked utterly devastated at the news. The vibrant temper that had made her look so magnificent, so indomitable, just moments before was gone.

Against his better judgment he stepped toward her, close enough to detect the citrus scent of the shampoo in her wild hair. "Can I make a suggestion?" he murmured.

She looked up at him, her green eyes like liquid pools of misery, reminding him of the girl she'd been five years ago. He'd crucified her then, for shattering his control. Recriminations swirled in his head now. He'd tried to put the blame for that episode on her at the time, because he'd never crossed that line before—not since he'd been a kid himself and controlling his urges had been impossible.

Neither of them was a kid anymore, though. And, if they were going to co-habit without giving in to the obvious chemistry between them, they needed to address the elephant in the center of the room. Or rather the dragon, he thought, as flames flared in his gut.

The thought of what she didn't have on under her robe tormented him—making it virtually impossible for him to keep his mind on their conversation, and not on the many things he had imagined doing to her all through the night after having her slim body plastered against his back on the ride to the villa.

He saw the flare of knowledge in her eyes, as if she had read his mind, before she tensed and stepped back. "I don't want you paying for my clothing," she said.

His temper kicked in. "Tough. It'll be days before the insurance money comes through," he said. "And you're not wandering around in a bathrobe," he added forcefully. "I'm not a saint."

Her eyes popped wide before a vivid blush suffused her face. Awareness crackled in the air around them like a physical force—and it occurred to him he might have made a tactical error admitting he wasn't immune to her. But he had assumed she knew. How could any woman not know, especially one as wild and reckless as her?

She looked genuinely shocked, though. Either that or she was an actress of Oscar-winning potential.

"I see," she said again, her slender neck moving as she swallowed.

Was her mouth as dry as his?

Did she have any clue how much he yearned to ease the drooping neckline of her robe the rest of the way off her shoulder and torment the elegant line of her collarbone with his teeth?

“If I accept the clothes…” Her labored breathing contradicted the stubborn set of her jaw. “I want to pay you back for them.”

*No way.*

“And I don’t need a ball gown—as I’m not going to any ball.”

He shoved his hands into the front pockets of his jeans, struggling to subdue his temper and the heat in his groin.

“I’ll allow you to pay for the clothes.” He’d have the stylist work out a reduced bill. “But only if you attend the ball with me.”

Her brows wrinkled. “Why do you want me to do that?” she asked, protesting a little too much. And he knew, however much she tried to deny it, she was as aware of him as he was of her.

While he knew that was not good news—because having an affair with Dario’s sister-in-law was the very last thing he had planned to do—his crotch didn’t seem to be in agreement.

“Honestly?” he said. “I don’t trust you to stay here unattended. And I have to attend to make sure the security operation is running smoothly.”

“You can’t force me to go with you,” she said, not denying she planned to bolt at the first opportunity. Her chin took on a belligerent tilt and he could see she was expecting him to try.

Anger burned at the evidence of her low opinion of him. He'd brought her here for her own good—and he wasn't in the habit of bullying women.

But then he recalled her testimony during Lloyd Whittaker's trial. And it occurred to him that her experience of men hadn't always been the best. It had come out loud and clear during the trial. Whittaker's attack on Megan had been the culmination of a long campaign of bullying and harassment against his elder daughter. At the time, Katherine's testimony had suggested she had been mostly spared because Whittaker had ignored her. But maybe the truth was more complex.

He knew what it was like to feel powerless and alone. Vulnerable in a way you couldn't defend against.

He pushed the unpleasant thoughts to one side. Not his business.

All he needed now was to get her cooperation.

"I'm not intending to force you to do anything," he said. "I'm not telling you, I'm asking you. I hate these damn events. You'll be doing me a favor." It surprised him to realize that wasn't far from the truth. However damned difficult the woman was, and however much of a temptation she presented, she was never dull.

He watched her consider his request, her arms tightening around her midriff, which had the unfortunate effect of plumping up her breasts beneath the robe.

"You'll definitely let me pay for the clothes when I leave?" she reiterated.

"Everything except the ball gown," he said, ignoring the implication that she wouldn't be returning to New York with him. He would correct that assumption later. "Have we got a deal?" he asked.

It took forever, but eventually she nodded. "Okay," she murmured, and she held out her hand to shake on it.

He closed his palm over her slender fingers. But then she looked down and flinched.

"What happened to your arm?" she blurted out.

He let go of her hand, drawing his arm away and tucking his fingers into the back pocket of his jeans.

His gaze met hers and he stiffened at the shadow of empathy in the luminous green.

He never hid the burns, not deliberately. They were a part of who he was, where he'd come from. A talisman, a symbol of how much he'd overcome to survive. But he didn't like her knowing he had once been at the mercy of circumstances beyond his control.

"It was an accident," he lied smoothly.

He could see she didn't believe him.

"I'll be back at seven," he ground out as he unclipped the helmet from the handle bars. "Be ready to leave at eight."

He climbed back aboard the bike. She didn't reply, but stood and watched as he kicked the bike off the stand and fired up the engine.

The unreasonable anger didn't make the desire still throbbing in his groin any easier to handle as he drove off.

* * *

Katie was questioning her impulsive decision to agree to Caine's request six hours later. Her newly manicured nails scraped on the beaded clutch purse that matched her gown, the afternoon now a blur of fabrics, fittings and design consultations.

She had been primped, preened, plucked and buffed to within an inch of her life in the last two hours, before Donatella and her team had finally left ten minutes ago. She assessed her appearance in the bedroom mirror. The blond tendrils dangling round her neck—which Sophia had spent an eternity teasing out of the chignon—gave her a sultry, just-out-of-bed look. The tension in her stomach twisted.

The smudge of black kohl and glitter round her eyes made the green of her irises pop, while the bronze silk dress—a retro fifties hour-glass style which she would never have contemplated wearing, given her less than abundant curves—actually made her look like she had a cleavage, with a little extra help from the push-up bra Donatella had insisted on.

"*You have curves—you just do not know how to flaunt them.*"

The simple ruched twist round the gown's bodice was perfectly complemented by the detailed sparkle of the jeweled beads sewn into the plunging neckline.

Katie let out a ragged sigh, the blond highlights in her hair caused by months spent under the Mediterranean sun glowed, set off by the final strains of the sunset through the open balcony doors.

Donatella had done her job far too well.

The plan had been to placate Caine and reduce the sexual tension between them until she had the means to leave. Not make herself feel like a lamb who had been dressed for slaughter.

*"I'm not a saint."*

The thought of Caine's eyes, the hunger she had seen reflected in the intense blue depths, sent another shudder of unease through her. She didn't want him to want her… That was what her rational mind was telling her. So why had every pulse point, every inch of skin, every single erogenous zone, rejoiced at the gruff confession?

She heard the murmur of voices in the villa's living area and her wayward pulse punched her neck, making the dusky light glimmer off the opals in her necklace.

She pulled her newly recharged phone out of the purse.

Eight o'clock on the dot.

Caine had arrived at seven as promised, according to the maid Inez, and had been getting dressed to take her to the ball… She stifled a slightly hysterical cough.

Jared was taking her under duress because he didn't trust her not to run off, and he had to go to the event for business reasons.

She needed to get her Cinderella complex under control.

Katie slipped her feet—fully recovered from yesterday's march after an hour-long pedicure—into the four-inch heels Donatella had picked out to go with her outfit. Tiny gemstones sparkled on the straps, but what should have looked trashy gave the outfit a funky, unique accent that chimed perfectly with what Donatella had insisted was Katie's rebel style.

Katie pressed her palms into the ruched silk covering her belly and strolled to the door—feeling about as rebellious as a church mouse.

*Suck it up, Whittaker. All you have to do is handle Caine for one night. And, anyway, this is not a date.*

Her steps faltered though as she walked through the living area and out onto the terrace—her pep talk floating off into the night as she spotted Caine standing in the dusk.

He wore a dark suit, perfectly tailored to his broad frame, and looked even more imposing than usual—a wolf in designer clothing waiting to pounce on its prey. Piercing sapphire eyes locked on her face. The punch of awareness hit her square in the solar plexus.

"Good evening, Katherine," he murmured. The rough cadence of his voice seemed to scrap over her nerve endings and she gripped the purse harder.

*Not a date. Definitely not a date.*

"Hi," she said, forcing her feet to move. Even wearing the four-inch heels she was several crucial inches shorter than him.

His gaze roamed over her outfit, making the push-up bra feel like an iron corset.

"I see you had a successful afternoon."

The husky tone only made her feel more insecure. The hint of a smile played over his lips again, adding an additional hitch to her breathing.

*Time to tough it out, Whittaker.*

Caine had no idea how inexperienced she was. She needed to play the part of a woman in charge of her own sexuality, or he would know exactly how much power he had over her.

"I'm glad you like it," she said, forcing the cocky confidence she had practiced for years in front of Lloyd Whittaker into her voice. "Seeing as it probably cost you a small fortune."

His leisurely gaze set off bursts of sensation over every inch of exposed skin. "I consider it a justifiable business expense."

His arrogance should have annoyed her, but the twinkle of wry humor in the startling blue eyes felt strangely beguiling, coaxing her to share the joke.

"I should warn you, not everything you see is real," she said, her own lips twitching. "The bra Donatello insisted on may well be worthy of a Nobel Prize for engineering."

His jaw tensed and the sparkle flared into something a great deal more potent, heating the warm night air.

"Good to know," he said in a tortured rasp that suggested the opposite. He glanced at the gold watch on his wrist. "We should go."

He rested his palm on the small of her back to direct her out into the hallway. She stretched against the proprietary touch, absorbing the giddy thrill.

The evening had settled in, the heady scents of the local wildflowers—jasmine and lavender and honeysuckle—hanging on the night air as he led her past the huge black motorcycle to the convertible he'd been driving on the mainland. The strange sense of disappointment—that she wouldn't have to wrap herself around that big body again—made no sense at all as he held the door open and she climbed into the luxury car.

A shiver racked her body as he folded his large frame into the driver's seat. For such a big man he moved with a fluid grace that made her think of a wolf again, or maybe a panther on the prowl. Big and powerful and predatory.

"Are you cold?"

She shook her head, unable to find her voice.

What was it about him that always seemed to leave her tongue-tied?

Five minutes later, Caine's sports car entered the grounds of a walled estate. Terraced gardens dominated by lemon groves and palm trees led down to a white Palladian mansion perched on the cliff top. The turn-of-the-century villa, which had once been owned by Italian nobility, had been refurbished to become the Venus Resort's hotel hub. It looked ethereal in the moonlight, a throwback to a bygone era, the elegant colonnades and intricate iron balconies illuminated by a series of flaming torches as the other guests arrived for the party.

A phalanx of press photographers stood behind a guide rope flanked by a security detail wearing the distinctive blue jackets of Caine Securities.

The knots in Katie's stomach yanked tight.

Caine got out of the vehicle and strode round to open the passenger door.

"What's wrong?" he asked.

She took his hand to step out of the car. "Nothing," she murmured, schooling her features as best she could, and wishing he wasn't quite so observant.

*Hold it together. It's not a problem.*

Caine's brows flattened, as if he were going to call her out on the lie. But then a young, heavy-set man wearing the Caine Securities uniform with his hand pressed to his earpiece approached them. "Signore Caine, the press are asking to be let into the venue."

Katie's pulse scrambled and Caine's hand settled on her hip. Could he sense her apprehension? Why did that make her feel more insecure?

"That's not the protocol for tonight, Marco," he said to his employee. "Remind them there's a full press conference tomorrow. Tonight's event is for the investors."

Almost as if Caine had sensed her distress, his hand firmed on her hip, forcing her closer to that seductive scent, making her aware of the hard lines of his body as they approached the entrance and the twenty or so photographers.

Flashbulbs fired in Katie's face and she stumbled. The visceral memory of another time, at her mother's graveside, and years later on the courthouse steps—when Caine's men had shielded her from the press once before, during her father's arraignment hearing—smacked into her like a fist.

Most of the shouts were in Italian, but then she

heard a nasally American voice cutting through the noise and slicing through the threads of her composure.

"Hey, if it isn't the naughty Whittaker sister. What you doing here, Katie? And where you been? We've missed you in New York."

She lifted her head, caught unaware, and saw a face she recognized. Jess Barton. One of the parasites who had trailed her relentlessly in the years after that court appearance, eager for a new scandal to photograph, another dumb stunt to document, so he could sell the evidence of her recklessness and immaturity to the highest bidder.

Clammy sweat dripped down her back, her gaze riveted like that of a deer in the headlights of an oncoming truck. Barton's eyes sharpened and he lifted his camera. A series of flashes blinded her and she jerked back. The flight instinct kicked in but, as if in a nightmare, her legs turned to mush, her feet caught in quicksand, and she stood frozen in place. Other paparazzi crowded around them, joining the feeding frenzy, as the flash of lights became an inferno of sound and fury.

"Back off." Jared's commanding voice boomed over her head and his arm banded round her midriff to keep her upright.

She swayed as his face—tight with anger—stared down at her. She had only a moment to register the diabolical pulse of heat and humiliation before he gathered her close and directed his men to hold the photographers back.

His muscular body shielded her from the shouts and demands. The blind panic retreated enough for her to draw in a breath as he propelled her up the villa's wide marble steps and into the huge vaulted entrance hall. She gulped in a lungful of clean laundry detergent and subtle pine soap.

Then she caught his underlying scent—rich, compelling and distinctly masculine—and the giddy wave of relief morphed into something much more disturbing.

Embarrassment scalded her cheeks.

"Please let me go. I'm fine." Forcing her legs to cooperate, she wrenched herself out of his arms.

She shouldn't want his support. Certainly shouldn't need it. She'd never liked the press, but she'd never had such a violent reaction before. Obviously a few months of anonymity had turned her into a wimp.

"Stop struggling," he growled, one firm hand still clamped on her hip.

Her thighs trembled as her stomach clenched against the disorientating heat.

A callused fingertip tucked under her chin and lifted her face. "Why didn't you tell me you have a phobia of the press?"

"Because I don't. I just wasn't prepared to see Barton here," she said, scrambling for an excuse, anything that would make her feel less exposed.

"The American?"

"Yes, he recognized me. The others didn't, I'm sure. I'm old news. Really, it's not a problem." She stepped back, mindful of their audience and the way

Caine was staring at her, as if he were seeing her for the first time.

"It looks like a problem to me—you're whiter than a ghost."

She tugged her elbow out of his grip. "Really, I'm fine. I just wasn't expecting to see the photographers here. Can we let it drop?"

A waiter swung past and she scooped a glass of champagne from the tray. She took two hefty gulps, willing her fingers to stop trembling as the chilly bubbles quenched the desert in her throat.

He was still watching her with that inscrutable look on his face.

Too unnerved to meet his gaze, she stared at their surroundings.

Men in tuxedos and dinner suits and women in designer gowns milled around them, dipping into the trays of canapés, sipping from champagne flutes, like exotic birds in a luxury zoo, many of them watching her and Jared with undisguised curiosity.

"I think I've made enough of a scene, don't you?" she asked, sipping more slowly. To think she'd once been a part of this world, briefly… She'd never felt more alien from it now.

"You didn't make the scene, they did," he said, the rough texture of his voice surprising her. He almost sounded sympathetic. Unfortunately it was a sympathy she knew she didn't deserve.

"They're just doing their job," she said.

"Their job is to take photos, not harass people," he said, the forbidding frown surprising her even more.

He clicked his fingers above her head and the well-built man who had spoken to them when they'd arrived appeared as if he were on a magic leash that Jared had just tugged.

"I want a photographer called Jess Barton escorted off the estate," Caine said to the young man. "Tell him his press pass has been revoked, and if I see any of the photographs he took tonight in print or on the Internet he'll be sued. Then inform the resort's PR and marketing team he's not to be readmitted under any circumstances. And tell Granger to draft a written warning to the others. I'll sign off on it tomorrow."

"Yes, sir, Signore Caine." The security guard nodded and then sped off to do Jared's bidding, as if such a request were perfectly normal.

Katie swallowed convulsively, the fruity bubbles of the champagne doing nothing to ease the emotion welling in her throat.

Why had Caine done that?

Surely he of all people believed the attention she got from the press was a justifiable penance for all the foolish things she'd done to attract their notice?

"You didn't have to do that," she managed at last, determined not to read too much into his actions.

"Yes, I did."

"But won't this jeopardize your contract with the resort's management?" she asked, even more confused and concerned for him. However rich he might be, and however successful his company, she did not want to mess things up for him because she'd freaked out over a few photos. "This is an investor's event—I'm sure they will want photos in the press."

His lips quirked, as if he thought her concern was somehow endearing.

"As I'm one of the resort's principle investors, the management works for me, not the other way around."

"Oh."

"But, anyway, that's beside the point."

"It is?"

"Yes. The purpose of this event is to gain investors, not to harass the guests. Barton stepped over the line."

"I… Okay." She drained the champagne, blinking back the foolish sting in her eyes.

She walked past him through the crowd, trying to get a grip on the foolish feeling of validation. Of support. She wasn't a child anymore, looking for approval, and Jared Caine certainly wasn't her father. It really didn't matter what he thought of her.

She took a moment to calm herself by absorbing the splendor of her surroundings. The building's starkly modern interior belied the eighteenth-century architecture. Polished marble floors added majesty to the domed atrium, where a winding staircase accessed a second level. The elaborate chandelier suspended from the ceiling several floors above was the décor's only nod to the building's history. Large double doors stood open, leading the guests onto a veranda that looked down over ornate terraced gardens.

A fountain dominated the main garden below

them, the elegant geometric pattern of lawns and hedges edged with a profusion of rose bushes, climbing vines and a series of grottos and follies which must have been part of the original layout.

A band played at the far end of the gardens. A dance floor had been laid out next to tables covered in white cloths and laden with crystal and silverware that sparkled in the torch light. A gazebo festooned with fairy lights and flowers sheltered the couples who were already making the most of the entertainment, dancing to the bass beat of the music. She dismissed the thought of dancing with Jared Caine, something she'd dreamed about often as a confused nineteen-year-old when she'd been looking for any distraction.

She didn't need distractions now.

But the whole scene looked foolishly romantic. And stupidly date-like.

Why hadn't she thought this through? She should have refused to accompany Jared tonight. And why had he wanted her to escort him, anyway? They were stuck together here because of his work—and his loyalty to Dario. But something had shifted when he had ordered Barton off the premises. Something she didn't know how to shift back.

She swung round as he came to stand beside her, his big body radiating tension. He lifted the empty champagne flute out of her hand and deposited the glass on the tray of a passing waiter. She felt the weird spell intensify, making them invisible to everyone.

"You don't have to hang out with me," she said. "I'll be fine on my own, if you need to mingle."

Why did she have to look so damned exquisite, and so vulnerable, while she was giving him the brush-off?

Jared watched Katherine's gaze flicker away. The glittery powder on her lids shimmered. He could see the flutter of her pulse through the skin of her collarbone, her cleavage drawing his eye as the slopes of her breasts pressed against the bodice of the beaded gown.

The feeling of connection was only made more disturbing by the visceral blast of longing.

He'd tried to convince himself he'd only escorted her to this event, so he could keep an eye on her while dealing with the hundred-and-one details that still needed his attention before the full press launch tomorrow. The hundred-and-one details he should have dealt with this afternoon instead of constantly checking with the villa staff that the styling team was keeping his uninvited guest occupied.

After she'd agree to accompany him, he'd left the villa this afternoon determined to keep things strictly impersonal this evening.

But the memory of her slender body wearing nothing but a bathrobe had continued to torment him throughout the day.

And then she'd stepped out onto the terrace this evening and the sight of her—her subtle curves accentuated by the glimmer of silk, her sultry eyes bright with bravado and provocation—had made the pulsing ache plunge straight back into his abdomen.

And he'd known the real reason he'd asked her to tonight's event—because every thought bar one had been incinerated by the firestorm of lust.

*I want her, no matter what the consequences.*

His groin had been keeping the faith ever since, the longing to rip off the silk gown and lick every inch of what lay beneath taking this afternoon's torment to a whole new layer of agony.

But he'd managed to yank himself back from the edge by repeating the same tired mantra to himself during the drive here.

Katherine Whittaker was a spoiled gold digger who didn't deserve a moment of his time. His irrational hunger now was simply a hangover from the unrequited need that the first taste of her had triggered five years ago.

He enjoyed sex. He was an accomplished lover. Not the boy he'd once been with desires he couldn't control.

He had destroyed that wild, feral kid years ago—buried him deep, while building a multinational business.

But he'd seen the blind panic flash in her eyes when that jackal had stuck a camera in her face. And the first tenet of his mantra—that Katherine was a spoiled gold digger—had collapsed.

She'd looked terrified. But instead of defending herself she'd blamed herself.

The next tenet of his mantra had soon followed suit.

Why did it matter if his hunger was triggered by what had happened—or almost happened—five years ago, if it was still as real and vivid today?

And now the third tenet was close to becoming toast too, because the driving need to touch, taste and torment her was telling him that while he might find it easy to control his need with other women it had never been easy with her.

"I don't need to mingle," he said.

"Don't worry," she said. "You can trust me not to run off. I doubt I could run anywhere in these heels."

"Can you dance in them?" he asked.

Her gaze lifted to his. "Yes, why?"

"If you recall, I paid a small fortune for that dress," he said, letting his gaze drift over the shimmering silk. "Which gives me certain privileges."

Taking her hand, he pressed a kiss to the thin skin at her wrist. Need bolted through him when she jolted.

Threading his fingers through hers, he turned and headed down the marble steps toward the gardens.

To his surprise, she didn't resist.

"Where are we going?" she asked breathlessly.

He didn't reply, because he didn't want an argument.

But he measured his steps and kept his grip firm as he weaved in and out of the other guests, then took one of the covered paths toward the dance floor in case she tried to bolt. The tiny lights embedded in the vines made it feel as if they were walking through a tunnel of starlight toward the low, pounding bass beat.

He quashed the romantic thought.

At last they reached the dance floor. He stepped onto the wooden boards and swung her into his arms. She grasped his shoulder to steady herself, allowing him to clasp her waist and tug her securely into his body.

Her soft curves yielded and the hunger that had been driving him since yesterday lunged. He moved easily to the music and she followed instinctively, for once allowing him to lead without an argument.

The pulsing beat in his abdomen became more insistent.

Damn, but he had always wanted to tame this woman. To hear that soft sob of need again which had come out of her mouth five years ago when he had lost himself in her kiss.

He knew he should fight the urge. She was Dario's sister-in-law—he was supposed to be protecting her until he could return her to the bosom of her family. Protecting her from men exactly like him, who only had the ability to take, never to give.

But with her body moving sinuously against his—the strands of her hair touching her neck where he wanted to feast on her skin, her deep, emerald eyes wary but the pupils dilated with arousal, the fairy lights flickering off the shiny gloss on those far too kissable lips—he was losing the will to care about anything but the persistence ache in his crotch.

Her hips brushed tantalizingly against the thickening ridge in his pants. And he absorbed the kick of adrenaline when her brows shot up her forehead.

"Caine?" she gasped.

"Perhaps you should call me Jared, in the circumstances," he murmured, amused despite himself by the shock on her face. "Don't look so surprised," he added. "You're a beautiful woman, Katherine. And I'm not a monk."

"I know," she said. "I can feel the evidence."

The bold statement, delivered with a refreshing lack of vanity or subterfuge, made a strange thing happen. He felt it bubbling inside his chest, like a volcano about to blow, and before he could contain it the laugh burst out of his mouth.

A smile split her face and suddenly her light, effervescent laugh was matching the deep chuckles reverberating through his chest, drawing the gazes of the other dancers.

The adrenaline surged.

When was the last time he had laughed at anything? Probably the last time he'd sparred with this woman. Back then she'd been volatile and reckless, reminding him far too much of himself at that age.

But tonight he couldn't seem to resist the urge to play with her. To provoke her the way she'd once provoked him. And take the vulnerability out of her eyes.

As their laughter died, her tongue flicked out to add moisture to the glossy sheen on her lips and the arousal which had subsided for a few precious seconds shot straight back to his crotch.

He groaned. Turning her in his arms, he pressed his hands to her shoulders and whispered against the soft hairs nestled under her ear, "I think we better get off the dance floor before I'm unable to walk."

"Okay," she said, her voice barely audible above the grinding pulse of the music.

He spread his fingers to press his hand to the bare flesh exposed by the dress's plunging back. His smile died as they made their way to the tables laden with a variety delicacies sweet enough to tempt even the most discerning palate.

"Are you hungry?" he asked.

She glanced at him and nodded. And somehow he knew neither of them was talking about food.

He handed her a plate then proceeded to pile it high with a selection of the delicate pastries, tarts and local cheeses on offer while struggling to quell the desire to taste those lips—to lick across the seam and demand entry.

He found them a seat on one of the vacant tables by the fountains, the music from the band complemented by the tinkle of running water.

The night was warm, so he took off his jacket and draped it over the back of his chair, then rolled up his sleeves, the white linen shirt suddenly feeling like a straitjacket.

She picked at the food, watching him as he sat down. She licked at a drop of olive oil and he forced himself to concentrate on his own food. But, as he swallowed a mouthful of Dolcelatte, the sharp, creamy taste did nothing to ease the hunger deep inside.

"I've never heard you laugh before," she said, breaking the silence and trapping him in the bold, green depths of her eyes. "You should do it more often."

Whether or not she meant the forthright statement to be beguiling, it was, especially when her teeth dug into that full bottom lip.

"I don't usually have a reason to," he said, which was the truth—he very rarely let down his guard, because he'd been taught at an early age not to.

"Or maybe you just take yourself too seriously?" she teased.

"Being me is a serious business," he countered, the urge to flirt back a novel one.

He didn't generally find much to amuse him in his relationships with women. Sex was a serious business. He didn't take it lightly, for the precise reason that he knew he must always hold a part of himself back.

"Why is that?" she asked.

He frowned, not sure what she was asking him.

But before he could think up an adequate reply—one which would deflect anymore too-personal questions—she leaned forward and touched the scars on his forearm.

"Is it something to do with these?" she asked. "How did you get them?"

The citrus scent of her shampoo filled his lungs, the smooth silk of her skin stretching taut over her lush breasts, and his usual caution when it came to conversations with women deserted him.

"My stepfather couldn't find an ashtray."

He heard her gasp of distress, her fingertips trembling on the old burn marks, and he wanted to drag the words back. Why had he told her that?

Why give her ammunition against him? And why bring up something that he had forgotten about a lifetime ago?

“That’s horrifying, Jared, I’m so sorry.” Her eyes became liquid pools of anguish and the emotion he thought he had conquered as a boy recoiled in his gut.

“Don’t be,” he said, the sharp bite of his tone making her blink. “I’m all grown up now.”

Twisting his forearm, he caught her wrist and tugged her closer. He didn’t want her sympathy. And he certainly didn’t need it. What he wanted was much more basic than that.

“And so are you.”

Pheromones fired through his brain, obliterating all thoughts of Dario and the promises he’d made, until all that remained was the driving need to taste her again.

He raised his hand slowly, giving her every chance to resist, and settled his palm against the soft skin of her cheek. The jog in her breathing was enough to make the heat slice through the last of his reservations.

His palm slid across the downy skin and his thumb located the well under her ear lobe. He rubbed back and forth, feeling her pulse flutter.

He waited a few beats then threaded his fingers into her hair. A tremble wracked her body and desire surged. He nudged her closer until their mouths were only a fraction of an inch apart.

He waited a beat, then captured her lips. She hummed deep in her throat and his resolve to be gentle got blurred by the surging need to conquer.

He licked, demanding entry, and tasted the tart hint of lemon *zabaglione*.

She opened for him on a sharp intake of breath and he cradled her face, anchoring her head to delve deep. Her hands dropped to clutch his waist, her fingers fisting in the linen of his shirt.

His tongue thrust and retreated, establishing a primal rhythm in a dangerous dance. Blood pooled in his abdomen and stiffened the erection which had been plaguing him all day. He heard the dull thud as the plate she'd had perched on her lap hit the grass. He focused on her taste, her texture, deafened by the throbbing pulse rushing past his eardrums as the blood charged into his crotch.

When he finally came up for air, she was panting. Her eyes fluttered open. As the haze of desire cleared, she jolted back, tearing her head out of his hands.

She touched shaking fingertips to her mouth, her delicate skin abraded by the light rub of his freshly shaven cheeks. She stood and scrambled back.

"That shouldn't have happened," she said.

He stood too, knowing he should agree with her but finding it hard to think past the hunger clawing at his gut. Because there was nothing more he wanted to do right now than take her back to the villa and carry her to his bed.

She picked up her purse, and pressed it to her belly, her head downcast as she chewed on her bottom lip. “I’d like to return to the villa alone,” she said, her voice so full of confusion and anxiety, it sparked his temper.

She couldn’t be innocent—he knew that. She was twenty-four years old and had spent the last five years busy collecting boyfriends as well as citations.

“No way,” he said. “I’ll escort you.”

Her eyes grew wide, and fury with himself edged his voice. “Don’t worry. I can keep my hands to myself.”

Did she think he was some kind of beast? Incapable of controlling his own hunger?

He texted Marco Calzone, the young Italian whom he had tasked with heading up tonight’s security detail.

Taking Katherine’s arm, feeling the pulse punch the inside of her elbow, he escorted her back through the gardens and up the marble steps toward the entrance hall. Marco was waiting with the keys to his convertible.

They drove back to the villa in silence.

She dashed off to her room, obviously concerned that he would try to follow her. Try to force himself on her.

He ought to return to the party. Forget about her. But the throbbing ache in his crotch refused to subside.

Disgusted with himself, and her, he walked through the villa then headed down from the terrace, through the gardens toward the pool.

He stripped down to his boxers and dived in. The frigid water stung his skin, finally cooling the heat that had been building ever since Katherine had walked out onto the terrace. The heat that had made him want to press her to his will.

He powered through the water, flipped into a turn and then powered back toward the deep end—ready to carry on going until he'd tamed the beast inside him. But he had a bad feeling that, now the damn thing had been unleashed, there would be no putting it back in its cage tonight, even if he swam all the way back to freaking Sorrento.

Katie flipped the lock on her bedroom door. But she knew it wasn't Jared Caine she was trying to keep out—it was herself. And her reaction to him.

The firestorm that had burned through her blood when he'd kissed her was everything she remembered from five years ago, and more. His lips had been coaxing, subtly demanding at first, but as soon as she'd opened her mouth she'd been plunged into a pit of red-hot lava.

If she'd been concerned about the strength of her attraction to him before, she was terrified now.

She crossed the room to fling open the balcony doors. The breeze went some way to cooling the burn on her cheeks until she heard the rhythmic splashing coming from the pool.

Walking onto the balcony, she leaned over and spotted Jared's powerful body slicing through the water in smooth, efficient strokes. Her breath got trapped in her throat as she watched him.

She shouldn't look.

But she couldn't seem to detach her gaze. Eventually, his strokes slowed, he braced his hands on the edge of the pool and lifted himself out. Water sluiced down his body as he kicked off the wet boxers. He was too far away for her to make out any details but she recalled the feel of him, his hard length pressing into her belly as they danced. She devoured the sight of him, so tall, so powerful as he walked across to the pool house and lifted a towel from the pile by the door.

He toweled himself in leisurely strokes then hooked the towel around his waist. He took the terrace steps two at a time then strolled through the gardens toward the villa.

She lurched back to plaster her body against the balcony wall, scared he would see her transfixed.

She crept back into the darkened bedroom but stopped dead as she heard the soft pad of his bare feet in the living area outside. The footsteps slowed, then stopped, and she noticed the shadow cast under her door.

Her heartbeat hit her larynx in harsh, staccato thuds. The urge to cross the room and fling open the door, to tell him how much she wanted him, held her spellbound. She felt terrified and aroused at the same time. But then the shadow faded away with the sound of his retreating footsteps.

Her breath released in a rush, her body sagging with relief.

She got ready for bed in a daze. But as she lay on the coverlet, staring at the beautiful plasterwork on the ceiling, the bed's drapes fluttering in the sea breeze, all she could see was the power and majesty of his naked body. All she could feel was his mouth on hers, forceful and demanding—and her body hummed, brutally captivated by the rich, fluid kick of exhilaration.

# CHAPTER FOUR

"YOU'LL DO AS I tell you or you'll rot here."

Visceral terror crawled over Jared's flesh as the vicious taunt hissed in his skull. The fetid smells—damp, vomit, rotting food—and the funky smell of stale sweat suffocated him. The pain burned and throbbed, pinpricks of agony.

He could see the crack of light beneath the door, could hear the deafening snap as the bolt drew back. The bones of his spine cracked against the wall as he scrambled away from the light, trying to make himself invisible. The pulsing glow of neon lit his stepfather's face and he morphed into a monster. Terror charged through Jared and he whimpered.

Punishing hands grabbed his arms, indescribable pain lancing up them, and the silent screams trapped in his throat burst free.

Jared jerked awake, yanked out of the nightmare by his own hoarse shouts. His ribs hurt from the violent panting. The sea breeze from the open terrace door chilled the pool of sweat dampening fine Egyptian sheets. The old marks burned, the paralyzing pain new and raw.

He jolted upright, throwing off the sheets. And sunk his head into his hands, his body shaking from the nightmare.

No, not nightmare—night terrors. That was what the therapist had called them.

Humiliation washed through him. Unable to control the tremors, like a drunk with the DTs, he staggered into the bathroom.

He should have closed the balcony doors before he'd gone to bed. What if Katherine had heard him screaming and whimpering like a terrified child?

He took a moment, dousing his face with cold water, until his pulse finally tracked out of the danger zone and his heart no longer felt as if it were about to explode out of his chest.

He swallowed, the dryness in his throat momentarily bringing back the tremors—reminding him of that boy, kept thirsty in the stultifying humidity to make him comply, to force him to… He shook his head.

*Lock the fear back in that room. Don't let it out.*

Returning to the bedroom, he dragged on fresh shorts and headed out into the villa's kitchen. He needed a cold drink.

Once he had gulped down a glass of water, and refilled it, he braced his hands on the countertop, forcing his knees to lock, the ringing in his ears making him scared he was about to faint.

That was all he needed now, to collapse in a heap.

A tiny sound had him lurching round, to see Katherine standing behind him, her eyes round with concern but her face fierce with determination—a large vase held aloft in her hands like a weapon.

She dropped her arms.

“Jared, I thought I heard yelling. Is everything okay?”

*Not exactly.*

His lips twisted. The sight of her—so fierce, so fragile—planning to fight any and all intruders was almost amusing, in a blackly comic way. He fought to stop himself from keeling over in front of her.

“Yeah. I’m good. Just had a bad dream,” he said, forced to tell her at least some of the truth. But then his gaze tracked over her. She wore a slip of a thing, the hall light silhouetting her curves and leaving very little to the imagination. He could see the slim slope of her hips, the subtle jut of her breasts, the dusky shadow of her nipples.

Arousal surged through him and his knees trembled for an entirely different reason.

“Go back to bed,” he managed.

“Are you sure you’re all right?” Katie asked. “What was the dream about?”

What kind of bad dream left you looking like you had been dragged out of your own grave?

The white scars caused by his stepfather’s abuse stood out against the tanned skin of Jared’s forearms.

But then her gaze lifted to his face. Arousal darkened the bright blue of his eyes.

The hum kicked off in her stomach, setting off a deep, pounding ache. And the fear and panic that had sent her running from him last night was comprehensively drowned out by the thick beat of desire. Of longing.

As he was wearing only his boxer shorts, she was able to see far too much of his glorious body, up close now and way too personal.

The color that had been drained from his face returned to his cheeks, the flush slashing high across his cheekbones.

Although her mind was yelling at her to run, to escape, she felt trapped by her own longing. The desire to look at him, to study every inch of firm, resilient, satiny skin, was more than she could bear. So she stood riveted to the spot, absorbing every detail as she studied the dark curls of hair surrounding flat brown nipples. The happy trail ran down through the ridged muscles of his six-pack to the band of his boxers, and the hint of springy curls contained by the sinews defining his groin.

Her mouth dried to parchment, as she noticed the ridge of his penis outlined behind black cotton—thickening and lengthening as she stared. The thrill shuddered down to her core and her gaze jerked back to his face.

"You need to go to bed before I finish what we started last night." His voice, rough with desire, seemed to stroke the swollen folds of her sex.

Despite his warning, the clear intent in his eyes, the panic refused to come, because all she could feel was the visceral blast of heat. Her nipples strained against the silk of her negligee, begging for the feel of those sure, sensual lips.

"I mean it, Katherine. I'm not kidding about." She could hear the barely leashed control in his voice, could see the feral light in his eyes. The veneer of sophistication had been ripped away, the ferocity of his desire evidenced by the heavy weight of the erection. His big body was restless and alive with tension, his ragged breathing matching her own.

"If you don't stay the heck out of my way for the next couple of days, I'm going to take what you offered me five years ago."

The growled ultimatum was a promise, not a threat. But the intent in his eyes, the flood of moisture between her thighs, jerked her out of the sensual trance. Her flight instinct finally kicked in.

Fumbling to put the vase on the edge of the counter, she turned and fled.

She raced to her room and shut the door. Her whole body shook, her clitoris throbbing. Sinking to the floor, her back hit the wall with a thud as she pressed her forehead to her knees and tried to make sense of the emotions, the needs careering through her system.

How could she be so enthralled by this man? She'd kissed other men before and since she'd kissed Jared Caine. But no man had ever had the ability to reach inside her and yank out that part of herself she'd kept hidden for so long. And the realization terrified her.

She couldn't be that woman, controlled by her desires. She didn't want to be that woman. A woman like her mother, with no morals, no loyalties. A woman ruled by her appetites and her own selfish pursuit of pleasure. Because then she would become everything she'd been running away from.

But Jared Caine had ignited the hunger she thought she'd tamed, like a volcano which had been lying dormant for five years, ever since their first kiss. And now he had blown all the lies she'd been telling herself to smithereens. During all her thoughtless escapades, all the dumb stunts and hijinks of the last five years, had she simply been attempting to replicate the thrill she'd only ever found in his arms?

She shivered despite the warm breeze from the balcony.

A tear tracked down her cheek and she brushed it away with her fist.

But as she forced herself off the floor and walked to the *en suite* bathroom on shaky legs, her thighs still trembling from the intensity of their encounter in the kitchen, she recalled the shouts from his room that had woken her up.

And she realized that, more disturbing than the sexual hold he had on her, were these glimpses behind the impenetrable shield of his emotions.

*Pull yourself together.*

So he'd had a tough childhood. And possibly still had nightmares about it. That didn't alter the fact he was a hard, uncompromising man, dominant and commanding, not the sort of guy she needed to get involved with.

Tugging off the negligee, she stepped into the

shower cubicle and turned on the water. She picked up the lemon-scented soap and began to scrub her skin, trying to wash away the memory of his gaze, the sizzle of anticipation still making her ache.

But as the lukewarm water sluiced over her she could still hear her breathless pants, feel his gaze on her tender flesh as the yearning continued to echo at her core.

She let her hand drift down to the wet curls at her sex and tried to feed the hunger. But her frantic efforts were stifled by a wave of shame—and terrifying longing.

Because beneath the fear of becoming like her mother, of giving in to the hunger that drove her, was the burning ache to feel him inside her. And the seductive knowledge that, however much she wanted to deny it, knowing he wanted her too was the biggest turn-on of all.

# CHAPTER FIVE

THE NEXT DAY Jared was gone again, busy working on the resort's press launch, according to Inez. After another sleepless night, her body tormenting her with images of him fully erect, the grumble of his warnings curling through her dreams, Katie convinced herself she was grateful. For once she planned to do as she was told and stay the heck out of his way for the duration of her stay.

Armed with her art box and a sheath of paper she'd found in the study, she headed through the gardens, ready to paint herself into exhaustion. They still hadn't dealt with the subject of what would happen once her passport arrived, but she had no doubt that Jared had simply assumed she would comply with Dario's wishes and accompany him back to New York.

That wasn't going to happen. As soon as she had her passport, she was heading back to Sorrento. But she would need watercolors to sell when she got there.

The sun was bright and punishing, the light glorious off the water as the tranquil turquoise sea lapped at the rugged coastline. Gnarled lemon trees shaded the path through the gardens, their pungent scent joined by the aroma of wild thyme and oregano. Steps etched out of the limestone led down to the villa's private cove, a sandy beach sheltered by shrubs and the glorious yellow flowers of the local broom plants.

Katie tried to clear her mind of all thoughts of Jared Caine, but even the stunning scenery failed to take away that deep ache which he had awakened the night before with a simple kiss.

In the distance, fishing boats and small tourist crafts sailed past the headland. She did detailed sketches then switched to watercolor, the small vignettes the perfect size for the gallery in Florence where she had sold her previous work.

But every time she tried to lose herself in her art the same questions kept torturing her.

What had Caine been dreaming about to make him cry out like that? And why couldn't she control her hunger for him?

The memory of Jared's body haunted her. The slopes and sinews of his muscular chest, as strong and indomitable as the cliff face...the dark intensity in his pure blue eyes as vivid as the translucent color of the sea.

The charcoal broke off in her fingers. And she swore under her breath, the now familiar heat flushing through her as she studied the drawing she'd sketched on autopilot.

She saw Jared Caine's face, his body, that glorious erection, so thick and heavy just for her, barely disguised by the cotton of his boxers. The desire to see him naked, to feel that warm, firm flesh in her hands, to lick every glorious inch of him like a drug, turned her body into a raw nerve.

She crumpled the sketch and stuffed it into her pack. Then scrubbed her hands over her sweat-slicked skin.

Was this what her mother had felt? Was this why she'd run away from Katie and Megan to join one of her lovers? Was this the giddy thrill which had been driving her when she'd put her life at risk that night on Capri and taken a high, fast drive with another of her many conquests after making love in the moonlight?

No wonder Alexis Whittaker had forgotten about all her responsibilities—her daughters, her husband, even her own safety.

Shouldering the heavy mahogany box of paints, brushes and sketching pencils, Katie made her way back up the cliff, more tired and out of sorts now than when she had arrived. Her whole body felt like a raw nerve begging for something it shouldn't want.

After the long, hot walk up the limestone steps, she trekked through the sheltered gardens, the trellises of flowering vines letting off a heady perfume as the sun began to sink toward the horizon.

The sound of slashing in the pool cut through her frantic thoughts and her pulse jumped as she spotted

Jared cutting through the water in powerful strokes, the setting sun gleaming on his dark head.

Instead of rushing back to her room, to hide out for another night, she toed off her sandals and stood transfixed in the shadow of an olive tree—unable to tear her gaze away from him. Just like the night before.

As he levered himself out of the water, moisture flowed over the sculpted muscles of his chest, flattening the smattering of hair. He reached for a towel and a small gasp escaped from her lips.

His head turned, and her heart charged into her throat. He watched her as he rubbed the towel over his chest in absent-minded strokes.

She stood trapped as the terrifying blast of heat consumed her.

Dumping the wet towel on a lounger, Jared stood with his legs akimbo, the stance deceptively casual. "What are you doing, Katherine?"

The low words felt like a caress on her too-sensitive skin, the burn of desire overwhelming her. A gust of wind made the short summer dress she wore press against her thighs.

"Watching you," she admitted.

"I thought I told you to stay out of my way?" His voice rasped across her skin like sandpaper.

"I've never been very good at taking orders," she said, forcing a defiance into her voice she didn't feel.

She wanted him, she wanted this, and she couldn't deny it any longer.

As scared as she was of taking this next step, she

was more scared of having him never look at her again the way he was looking at her now. As if he knew exactly what she wanted, what she needed. And knew how to give it to her.

One dark brow rose at the provocative statement, and she felt the surge of confidence. If there was one thing she'd always been good at, it was bluffing. Pretending not to care when she did care. Pretending not to be hurt when she was. Pretending to know what she was doing when she didn't have a clue.

Surely this was one time that being her mother's daughter ought to work to her benefit?

He pressed his hand to his jaw and rubbed the rigid muscles through the shadow of stubble, as if considering his situation. Their situation. But the fierce hunger in his eyes was unmistakable.

"If we do this thing, you need to know it means nothing to me," he said. "I don't do emotional attachments."

*Why?*

The word hung in the air as her gaze tracked to the scars that peppered his forearms. Emotion tugged at her abdomen, combining with the heat as the cries that had wrenched her from sleep the night before, those broken shouts ragged with agony, echoed in her head.

But she forced her gaze back to his face—and saw the challenge in his expression. He was daring her to ask, so he could have an excuse to leave her wanting.

She swallowed down the yearning to know more about him.

*Not your business.*

"I'm not great with emotional attachments either," she said, wishing it were true. "Just ask my sister—or Dario."

He huffed out a laugh, breaking the tension between them. "Fair point."

Stepping toward her, he lifted his hand. Slowly, carefully he cupped her cheek, the way he had the night before, as if he were giving her the chance to pull back. But this time the flight reflex refused to come. The chilled skin of his palm felt rough against her skin. He stroked his thumb over her lips. And her breath gushed out on a tortured sob, the coil in her belly yanking tight as the fire in his eyes flared.

"You're so damned exquisite." The gruff statement sounded as if it had been wrenched from him—and was all the more devastating because of it.

No man had ever looked at her the way he did. As if he wanted to punish her and worship her at one and the same time. That bold, unapologetic gaze, so full of longing, had a heady effect.

She had always needed to fight for every scrap of affection, had needed to shout to be seen, but with Jared it had always been different. He made her feel fully visible, fully present, fully alive—without her having to do anything at all. Except be.

Capturing her other cheek, he framed her face, then covered her lips with his. His tongue demanded entry, the kiss hard, punishing, hungry.

She opened for him instantly, her hands grasping his waist, the damp skin smooth and hard. She sucked on his invading tongue, letting the excitement sizzle through her body. He angled her head to delve deeper, to take more, his fingers driving into her hair, dislodging the band that held it back from her face.

The kiss was all she remembered from the night before and from all those years ago, and more, not coaxing this time or fleeting, but savage and demanding.

One large hand covered her breast. The nipple pinched into a tight point beneath cotton and lace.

He reared back, his face dark with desire as he stared down at her. "Are you sure? Tell me now, damn it," he demanded. "Because once I get you naked I'm not going to stop."

She nodded, every inch of her skin alive with sensation. "Yes. I'm sure."

He grunted then, bending, lifted her into his arms. She gasped, circling her hands around his neck, her stomach swooping into her throat as he strolled across the gardens, up the steps and then marched across the terrace.

Nudging open his bedroom door, he dropped her onto her bare feet. The room was larger than hers, the bed less fanciful, and unlike her own room everything was in perfect order, so pristine it was as if no one stayed here.

"Turn around," he said.

She did as she was told, and heard the sibilant rasp of the zipper as he yanked it down. Then the click as her bra released.

He hooked his fingers beneath the straps and she

found herself naked to the waist, the cotton dress slipping over her hips and her bra sliding down her arms. His callused palms covered her naked breasts.

She sunk against him, her knees buckling as he plucked at her nipples, the fire arrowing down. She could feel the hard length of him pressing against her lower back through the damp swimming trunks as his lips settled on her collarbone and he sucked the pulse in her neck.

Her ragged breathing sounded harsh in the quiet room. He turned her to face him and she crossed her hands over her breasts, a wave of insecurity assailing her.

"Don't," he said, his voice gruff as he took her wrists in his hands and tugged her arms away from her body. "Don't hide from me."

The sun was sinking beneath the cliff top, sending shards of light and shadow through the room, but she felt far too exposed. All the excitement of moments ago faded as he studied her. No man had ever seen her naked before. As a model, she'd refused to go topless. She'd avoided looking at herself in magazines, or on billboards, her boyish figure perfect as a designer clothes horse, but less so as a woman.

He tucked a knuckle under her chin, forcing her to look at him.

His jaw was hard as granite, the hunger still vivid on his face. "Are you shy?"

She shook her head. "No, I just..." Her excuses stalled.

The excruciating tension stretched tight, her

breasts still throbbing from his attention. The nipples distended under his gaze.

Lifting his thumb, he stroked the underside of one breast, circling the sensitive flesh, making it pucker into a hard point.

"Just what?" he asked absently, all his concentration on the play of his thumb over her nipple.

"I'm just not very well-endowed," she managed on a strangled gasp as he plucked at the peak until the blood rushed into the tortured tip.

"So what?" he asked, then bent his head and drew the tight peak into his mouth.

She grasped his head, holding him to her as the suction sent an exquisite drawing sensation straight to her sex.

She cried out soft sobs of protest and encouragement, the blood rushing to her engorged nipple as he transferred to the other peak and proceeded to torment it too with his tongue and his teeth.

When he finally lifted his head, she was barely able to stand. Hooking his finger into her panties, he dragged them down. She stepped out of them as he knelt before her, her legs shaking, her hands gripping the bunched strength of his shoulders for balance.

Then to her astonishment he grasped her buttocks in large palms and pressed his face to her sex, breathing in.

"You smell incredible."

She shuddered, unable to speak or breathe as he used his thumbs to open her up and then licked through the slick, swollen folds. The shocking intimacy made her jolt, but what shocked her more was the pulsing pleasure that rippled through her body with startling intensity as he teased her with his tongue. One blunt finger worked its way into her sex.

She groaned deep in her throat, shaking so much she felt as if she were dissolving into a pool of aching, unbearable pleasure. The loss of will frightened her—she felt as if she were in a trance her decisions no longer her own, her body drugged by his expert caresses.

Withdrawing his attentions abruptly, he stood and pressed her back onto the bed.

She lay down as he directed, surrendering to the carnal hunger. She wanted to cover herself again but she couldn't seem to move, trapped by his fierce, feral gaze. She drunk in the sight of him as he drew the wet swimming trunks down the long muscles of his thighs.

The erection sprang free, thick and long, curving toward his belly button. Her breath seized in her lungs, the sight of him both magnificent and intimidating.

He was large, much larger than she had anticipated. She longed to feel him thrusting deep, but wondered at her own hunger for the pain she knew it would cause. Pain she couldn't show him, or he'd know. He was her first. Her only.

He climbed over her, caging her in. Her body quaked as the thick erection brushed her hip.

"You're trembling," he said, cradling her face in

his palm, stroking her hair back with his thumb to brush it behind her ear. "Is something wrong?"

"No, nothing," she lied. "Can I touch you?" His brows furrowed and she stiffened at her own stupidity.

She couldn't have sounded more gauche and inexperienced if she'd tried.

"You don't have to ask my permission," he said. Taking her hand, he wrapped her fingers round the length of him.

Giddy joy raced through her as his erection leapt to her touch. She watched enthralled as he let her explore with tentative strokes. He felt soft and yet so hard, a drop of moisture appearing like a jewel at the tip. The deep, drawing sensation at her center turned to pulsating need.

"Enough," he said, drawing her hand away.

Reaching past her, he fumbled for a moment in the bedside drawer then produced a condom. She noticed the slight tremor in his fingers as he tore the foil then rolled the protection over the powerful erection. Did she affect him as much as he affected her?

He held her hips and she grasped his shoulders, opening to him, all her senses, all her needs, now focused on the coil deep in her abdomen.

She felt the blunt tip probing at her sex. He grunted, pressing inside her. Her flesh stretched, so tight, too tight, but then he thrust deep. And pulsing pleasure turned to rending pain.

She choked out a cry, heard his curse as he stilled.

He felt huge inside her, too huge, overwhelming her.

She bit into her lip, trying to relax, hoping he hadn't felt the small barrier tear, desperate for the bright, beautiful pleasure which had seemed so close moments ago to return.

She wiggled her hips, trying to ease the immense discomfort.

"Don't move," he said, his voice strained, rough with desire.

"Please don't stop," she whispered.

He raised his head and searched her face. Color lanced into her cheeks.

*He knows.*

She grasped his back, scared he was going to withdraw, going to leave her there, on the brink of something amazing. But then he began to move, sliding even further, stretching her even more.

She arched into the pain, as he notched a place deep inside. The shock of ecstasy ripped through her. Exquisite pain merged with merciless pleasure as he rocked against that place.

Her eyes closed, her breath coming in ragged pants, her body moving with his as he pulled out and drove deep, establishing a brutal rhythm. The waves of pleasure undulated, eddying upward, coiling tight, thrusting her into a maelstrom.

She heard his grunts, her sobs, his smooth, fluid movements becoming disjointed, savage. Sweat slicked their bodies, her fingers slipping against his skin as she tried to gain traction, gain momentum, clinging on for dear life, scared of falling, scared of letting go. Then the pleasure smashed into her, stealing her breath, forcing her over that bright, burning edge into shattering, soul-destroying oblivion.

*What the hell have you done?*

The accusations came from another dimension, whispering through Jared's dazed brain as his body came down from the mind-blowing orgasm.

He managed to lock his elbows, shaking through the final throes of the stunning climax, determined not to collapse on top of her. He pulled out of the exquisite clasp of her body, feeling as if he were leaving what little was left of his soul behind him.

She'd been innocent.

The memory of her artless, eager response to every caress blasted through him and he flinched.

He felt hollowed out, weighed down, as he rolled away from her to stare dumbly at the ceiling.

All the clues had been there. If he'd been paying attention to anything other than his own lust he would have realized the saucy come-on she'd given him by the pool had all been an act long before he'd plunged into her with all the force and fury of a battering ram.

The way she had wrapped her arms over her nakedness. The panicked look when she'd first laid eyes on his erection. The tentative request to touch him that he'd assumed was some kind of tease. The agonizingly careful way she'd caressed him. Every single one of those gestures made him think now of the kid she'd been five years ago.

Vulnerable and alone.

He'd taken advantage for a split second back then. He'd taken much more now.

Why had she waited so long? And why the heck had she chosen him?

He left the bed without looking back and headed for the bathroom. He needed a moment. The desire to apologize, to hold her and comfort her was almost as disturbing as the need already tightening in his groin, because he wanted to take her again, to stake his claim.

He got rid of the condom, horrified anew at the evidence of her innocence, then forced himself to return to the bedroom. Had he hurt her? He must have. She'd been incredibly tight.

But when he walked in she was crouched over, gathering up the dress, panties and bra where he had discarded them.

She bolted upright, gathering the clothing to her chest. Desire pulsed in his groin and he felt himself getting hard again.

"What are you doing?" he asked, more harshly than he had intended.

"Going back to my own room," she said, her voice a little shaky, but that stubborn chin jutting out the way it always did when she was trying to pretend she was tougher than she actually was. "I know you don't want me here."

If only that were true, he thought ruefully, it would make this so much simpler.

Her eyes darted down to his crotch, and he could see she'd gotten the message when her cheeks brightened with color.

*Yeah, precisely.*

He crossed to the dresser, tugged out a pair of clean sweatpants and put them on. And willed his libido to behave itself.

She hadn't moved, her long limbs vibrating with tension. She looked like a fawn, waiting for him to pull out a rifle and shoot her on the spot.

He almost winced, not a great analogy, given what had just happened.

"Why didn't you tell me?" he asked, trying to stay calm.

She simply stared at him. But the color in her cheeks went radioactive.

"That I was your first," he prompted. She couldn't have looked more guilty if she'd been a bank robber caught on the threshold of a vault with a bag marked "swag" gripped in her hands instead of a summer dress and lacy panties.

"I...I didn't think it was significant."

He stared her down, making it crystal-clear he wasn't buying that argument.

"And I didn't want to put you off," she added, all but choking on her embarrassment.

Given the pulsing ache in his crotch at the sight of her, he wasn't sure it would have, which only disturbed him more.

"Did I hurt you?"

She shook her head. "No."

"Don't lie," he said, taking a fresh bathrobe out of the closet.

Walking to her, he wrapped it around her shoulders and felt the tremor of response. The toweling engulfed her.

"Put it on," he murmured, tugging her clothes out of her hands and dumping them onto a chair.

She shoved her arms into the garment and tied the belt, her fingers visibly shaking with the effort to hide her nakedness as quickly as possible.

"Really, it didn't hurt that much," she said. "I enjoyed it." He wasn't sure he believed her, not entirely—he'd heard the gasp of pain when he'd ploughed into her—but her obvious urge to make him feel better about the whole thing beguiled him in a way he wasn't sure he liked.

He'd said he didn't do emotional attachments during sex, but apparently he did. With her. Because he felt responsible—for her pleasure, or rather the lack of it. And as if he had something important to prove that he'd never had to prove before.

"I could have made it more enjoyable," he said, touching a finger to her cheek. He stroked the soft skin, captivated by the wariness in her eyes and the instinctive tremor of reaction. "If you'd told me what was going on. I would have been a lot gentler."

Or he would have tried to be. Given the hunger that was already tearing at his gut again, with her quivering and blushing in front of him in nothing but a bathrobe, he wasn't so sure.

"I should go back to my room," she said, then went to walk past him.

He should have let her go. He wanted to let her go. But instinct took over and he grasped her shoulders, pulling her round to face him.

"You don't have to go," he heard himself say.

"You're not mad with me?"

He was more mad with himself. So he shrugged, the movement stiff and forced. He didn't want to feel responsible, but somehow he did. "You should have told me," he said. "But it was your choice not to."

Her shoulders relaxed and that stubborn chin sunk back to her chest.

She looked so confused—so devastated. And, whether he'd intended it or not, he was the cause.

"Come back to bed," he said, finally giving into the unprecedented urge to hold her. At least for a little while.

Her head lifted, the blush firing back across her cheeks. "I don't think…" She stammered, her gaze darting to the rumpled sheets. "I don't think that's a good idea, I'm a little…" She sighed. "Well, a little sore, frankly."

He chuckled, the sound harsh and strained, but easing at least some of the tension churning in his gut.

Damn, what was he going to do with this woman?

He had never found innocence a turn-on before. But he had to admit with Katherine it had always been a factor. The woman was a mass of contradictions—bold and provocative one minute and then strangely unsure the next.

Was that why she had always fascinated him?

Solving puzzles had always given him a rush. It was one of the things that had driven him to set up his own security agency—once Dario had hauled him out of the gutter and shown him a better way. It was a beautiful irony that the skills he'd learned on the street had eventually helped to make him a model citizen—and a very rich man.

Perhaps his fascination with Katherine was nothing more than an extension of that.

She'd always frustrated and intrigued him—even as a mouthy nineteen-year-old. Add in the insane sexual chemistry that had just flared out of control and it created a potent cocktail.

"What's so funny?" she asked stiffly, confusion and insecurity replaced by indignation, which only captivated him more.

"I'm not going to make love to you again tonight," he said. Or not in a way that would make her more sore, he corrected himself. He couldn't make any guarantees he would be able to keep his hands off her entirely.

"I just want to make sure you're all right."

The blush softened, and her eyes were shadowed by surprise, but also an emotion that struck him deep in the chest. Gratitude.

*Why would she settle for so little?*

His ribs tightened. He ignored the feeling. Plumping the pillows against the headboard, he lay down beside her and slung his arm around her shoulder.

She snuggled close to his side, resting her head on his arm, the shuddering sigh full of relief. He wasn't a snuggler—he never cuddled after sex because he'd never seen the point. But once again he found himself beguiled, oddly humbled by the ease with which she had accepted his comfort. Why would she trust him, he wondered, when he was the opposite of trustworthy where she was concerned?

She pressed a hand to his chest and wound her fingers absently in the hair there. The familiar heat triggered in his groin.

He flattened his hand over hers. "Go to sleep," he heard himself say, the selflessness of the gesture surprising even him.

There were so many things he still wanted to do to her. And so many questions he wanted to ask. But he remained silent, knowing the answers might deepen the strange sense of connection.

As she relaxed against him in sleep, the robe fell open, giving him a tantalizing glimpse of one flushed breast, the nipple rouged by his earlier attention.

The need pooled in his groin, intensifying the ache, the urge to draw the rigid peak into his mouth again and suck the same livewire response from her all but unbearable. But instead of waking her up, and bringing them both to another shattering orgasm, he found himself lying there in a state of purgatory and staring at the night sky through the terrace doors.

He had a golden rule, a rule he had never broken before now, had never even had the desire to break. He never slept with any woman for more than one night. But he already knew one night with Katherine would never be enough.

# CHAPTER SIX

KATIE AWOKE THE next morning with a start to find herself alone. In her own bed. Sights, sounds and sensations bombarded her from the night before. She might almost have believed it was another erotic dream as she lay in the bright, airy room, the sun streaming through the balcony doors, but for the tenderness between her thighs and the oversize bathrobe she was still swaddled in.

Jared's mouth hot on her breast, his penis hard and thick as he entered her, the all-consuming orgasm which had swept through her… And afterward the shock, the concern and—so much more devastating to her peace of mind—that tantalizing glimpse of the man behind the facade.

For a moment as he'd held her afterward she'd felt so secure, so safe.

She blinked, the sting of tears in the back of her throat almost as concerning as the melting sensation in her core.

She crawled out of bed and headed to the bathroom as numerous other niggling aches and pains made their presence felt. The scalding-hot shower went some way to restoring her equilibrium, or at least a semblance of it. But she still felt off-kilter.

She'd spent so long trying to suppress her mother's legacy that on some weird subliminal level she'd simply assumed she would be able to sleep with Jared and forget about it. The way her mother had done with so many men.

The vague recollection of him carrying her back to her own room, and her sleepy attempts to get him to stay, made her shiver as she soaped her hair and tested the tenderness in her breasts.

How could she not have realized sex would be so…well, so intimate?

She tugged on a pair of shorts and a T-shirt, the shaky feeling returning as she recalled the look on Jared's face when he'd come back out of the bathroom.

If she was reluctant to need a white knight, Jared was considerably more reluctant to be one.

The questions that had taunted her yesterday night swirled back into her brain.

Why didn't he do emotional attachments? Quite apart from anything else, didn't he get unbearably lonely?

While she'd always shied away from sexual intimacy, she'd found it incredibly hard to live without emotional intimacy, especially in the last few months.

How many times had she had to resist calling the De Rossis, homesick for the sound of Megan's voice, Dario's gruff advice, or Izzy's inane prattle about unicorns, Disney Princesses and her latest Lego construction? How many times, particularly in the first few weeks, had she latched on to groups of people because being completely alone had terrified her? People like the German backpackers she'd partied with for one glorious weekend after meeting in an Amsterdam hostel. Or the bar staff in Paris she'd hung out with every night after lights out while working for a few weeks in a Bastille brasserie.

If anything, being alone had made her appreciate so much more the company of others.

A pang dug into the center of her chest. Why would anyone commit themselves to a lifetime without those connections if they didn't have to?

Hot on the heels of that thought came the memory of Jared's caresses, so urgent, so addictive. Heat spiraled down to her core—the yearning acute, despite the soreness still lingering in her sex, and making her blush when Inez brought in a breakfast tray.

There was a folded note propped up against the coffee pot with her name written on it in Jared's thick black scrawl.

Katie forced herself not to grab it off the tray but she couldn't control the kick of anticipation as the maid poured the coffee and arranged a dish laden with frittata and ham on the balcony table. The tempting scent made her empty belly growl.

As soon as Inez had left the room, Katie lifted the note and flicked it open.

Her heart beat an uneven tattoo as she scanned the three short sentences.

*Last night shouldn't have happened. It won't happen again. I'm not in the habit of deflowering virgins.*
*Caine*

Her heart sunk into the pit of her stomach and the paper fluttered to the floor from nerveless fingers. The warmth, the feeling of safety and security, even the insistent buzz of sexual arousal, was replaced by the sharp stab of hopelessness and inadequacy.

"Everything's good, Dario. The passport should be here by Monday," Jared spoke into his cell phone, his voice hoarse as the guilt threatened to strangle him.

He'd had another nightmare last night. Had woken up aching and sweating, his head splitting, the terror so huge his throat had been raw from the shouting—and his penis as hard as an iron spike. Because in his nightmare Katherine had been locked in that squalid room with him.

Thank God he had remembered to close the terrace doors this time before falling into a restless sleep.

He had spent the morning immersed in a conference call with the San Francisco office at the resort's business center and harassing his PA to get onto the British consulate again and get an answer out of them about the ETA on Katherine's passport.

It hadn't helped. Instead of calming him down, he now felt even more shaky and tense.

"Jared, is there a problem?"

He thrust an impatient hand through his hair, clinging on to his usual cool by his fingertips as he recalled the sweet, seductive light in Katherine's heavy-lidded eyes as he'd placed her in her own bed the night before.

*Can't you stay with me?*

"It's nothing," he said down the phone line. "I guess I'm just tired and kind of stressed." Not surprising, given that he hadn't had an uninterrupted night's sleep since Katherine had burst back into his life. "The Borelli buyout was more complicated than I thought," he added.

He heard Dario's wry chuckle. "Owning and operating a billion-dollar company sucks sometimes, no?"

Jared let out a strained laugh.

If only that were the problem.

A loud rap sounded on the door and he ended the call with Dario as he beckoned his executive assistant into the room. The efficient young man looked agitated, which was not like him.

"What's wrong, Carlo?" he snapped, the little patience he had left evaporating.

"The villa's housekeeper has called. She says Ms. Whittaker left the premises without telling anyone and that she borrowed the gardener's scooter."

Jared's heart hit his tonsils. "When?"

"About half an hour ago."

He swallowed down the curse, the frustration caused by Dario's call coalescing into something a great deal more volatile.

Shouting instructions to the young man to have five of his men sent to Marina Grande, Capri's main port, in case Katherine attempted to leave on the ferry, he strode out of the building.

As he mounted the bike and peeled away from the resort offices, his temper kicked in—but did nothing to override the wave of panic and concern.

He'd planned to create some distance today, for both their sakes, to give them time to get over last night's mistake and control the hunger once and for all.

Trust Katherine to screw up his best laid plans.

# CHAPTER SEVEN

THE ROAR OF the motorbike's engine drowned out the putter of the tiny Vespa. Katie's head whipped round and her heart charged into her throat as Jared's monstrous black bike drew alongside. He signaled her to stop. Reluctantly, she braked on the deserted road.

*Seriously? Can this day actually get any worse*?

Stopping the bike in a spray of stones, Jared dragged off his helmet and dismounted. He stalked toward her, brushing back disheveled locks of dark hair. With his suit pants speckled with dust and his white shirt sticking to his chest in damp patches, he looked more untamed than she had ever seen him. As his big body bore down on her, the memories from the previous night came flooding back unbidden, dark and torrid, and only added to her humiliation. She forced herself to stand her ground as the shock of awareness reverberated through her system.

His head dipped. Even hidden behind the dark lenses of his sunglasses the heat of his gaze burned over every inch of exposed skin—which unfortunately was quite a lot in her T-shirt and shorts.

"Where the hell do you think you're headed?" The growled demand had her temper kicking in at last, smothering the crippling pain caused by his note.

"I didn't know I was under house arrest."

He tore off his sunglasses and fury sparked in his deep-blue eyes.

"You spoiled brat! I've just spent the last half hour searching the island for you."

The old insult stoked a restorative wave of fury.

"Why would you bother?" she snapped. "You've already deflowered me, remember?"

The insensitivity of his note cut her to the bone all over again. He'd destroyed her in that moment, the same way he had five years before. The same way her father had every time he'd made her feel small and insignificant. But she refused to be beaten down. Or ashamed of what she'd given freely and openly the night before. And the pleasure they'd shared.

He stiffened, obviously taken aback. "The note was supposed to be an apology for that."

"If that's your idea of an apology, you need a lot more practice."

And did he really think an unnecessary apology was going to make her feel any better?

"Fine, I'll say it again," he ground out through gritted teeth. "I'm sorry about what happened last night. If I had known it was your first time, I would never have touched you." He thrust his hand through his hair, making deep grooves in the sweat-soaked waves. If she hadn't been so miserable, she might have taken some satisfaction in knowing she had finally blasted through his usual cool. "And you were the one who chose to keep it a secret."

"Don't you get it?" she asked. "I don't need or want an apology. I *wanted* to make love to you. I made a choice. That I don't regret. Even if you do."

A choice she was now determined to own once and for all with this morning's excursion, if she ever managed to find the place she'd been searching for in the dusty heat for over an hour.

"Oh, yeah? Then why the hell were you running away from me?" he asked, exasperated.

She stared at him, stunned by the passion in his voice. Seeing past her own unhappiness for a moment, she realized that more than impatience and temper lurked in his gaze.

But the thought he might be genuinely concerned for her failed to compute. Hadn't she fallen down that rabbit hole the night before? And look what it had cost her. He didn't care about her. The only reason he had shown her any consideration yesterday was through some warped sense of responsibility for her inexperience. And the only possible reason he could have for haring after her now was his dogged obsession with keeping the promise he had made to Dario.

"I wasn't running away," she murmured, suddenly weary of the argument, and clinging desperately to her composure. "I have somewhere I wanted to go."

Because there was something she had always refused to confront and the events of last night—and this morning—had finally given her the courage at least to try.

He swore under his breath, his frustration clear. "Uh-huh? Well, next time you decide to steal a scooter and go joyriding, let Inez or one of the other staff know so I don't have to interrupt my day to come looking for you."

"I didn't steal it, I was going to bring it back." Outraged color tinged her cheeks at the injustice of the accusation and the patronizing tone. Would he ever stop treating her like an irresponsible child? She was twenty-four years old and last night she had finally felt like a grown woman for the first time in her life. But he was determined to take even that away from her. "And I didn't tell anyone where I was going because I didn't want anyone to know." *Especially you.*

Although, she could see the folly of that decision now. Maybe she should have taken a moment to ask Inez for directions, because she'd been traveling up and down the walled roads and deserted tracks on this side of the island and she had yet to find her first graveyard. Not knowing the word for cemetery in Italian certainly hadn't helped. But after reading his note she hadn't really been thinking at all, she'd simply been reacting to the hurt and confusion his curt dismissal had caused. And that was the thing that angered her most of all—not with him but with herself.

When was she going to learn to stop being so impulsive? And when was she going to stop letting the low opinion of men like Jared and her so-called father Lloyd Whittaker matter to her? She thought she'd come so far in the last few months by surviving on her own and pushing herself to be resilient and self-sufficient. But Jared had managed to turn all that hard work on its head with one stunning orgasm, a few unexpected hugs and three thoughtless sentences.

She felt as if she had been slapped back to square one after a particularly brutal game of Chutes and Ladders. The thought that she might never be ready to return home to Manhattan, that she might never be more than Megan's troublesome little sister, suddenly crippled her with anxiety.

"Where could you possibly have to go on an island you don't know that's important enough to put the whole villa, not to mention my business, in uproar?" Jared snarled, still channeling an enraged mountain lion who'd been poked once too often.

"I wanted to visit my mother," she blurted out.

One dark brow shot up—the temper tantrum momentarily stopped in its tracks. "Your… Who?"

"Alexis Whittaker," she clarified, already regretting her outburst. Which was just one more sign of her inability to think straight when cornered. "She's buried somewhere on this island," she added when he continued to stare at her as if she had lost her mind. "I came here once before. The winter we buried her. It's one of the reasons I didn't want to come back."

Although not the biggest reason. Because that was standing right in front of her, stunned into silence for once. "It's not a particularly good memory. But I thought I'd be able to find it. That I'd remember the graveyard…if I saw something familiar." She was rambling now but she couldn't seem to stop, his indomitable presence making the whole idea begin to seem even more foolish. What was she even trying to do—get validation for her actions from a woman she had never even known and who had been dead for years?

"But nothing looks familiar," she said, finally winding down. "Probably because it's high summer now. And at the time I was only eight."

He didn't say anything for the longest time. He just stared at her as if he were trying to solve a particularly complicated riddle.

She felt the last of her anger drain away until all that was left was the foolish girl who had woken up this morning and believed that something good had happened last night. She wasn't a romantic and, despite her inexperience, she wasn't naive either, so she hadn't kidded herself what she had shared with Jared was more than sex. But still, finding the courage finally to make that physical connection with someone had meant something to her. Something she'd been dumb enough to believe had been awesome enough for both of them to be repeated. And the way he'd held her afterward had made her feel noticed, even cherished, by a man for the first time in her life.

That it had all been an illusion—conjured up by heat and pheromones—only made her feel more exposed.

He was probably trying to figure out why she would want to visit her mother's grave, but she didn't intend to enlighten him. Especially as she wasn't even entirely sure herself.

"Was your mother a Catholic?"

Katie frowned at the non-sequitur, and the intensity on his face. If only she could read him as easily as he seemed to be able to read her.

"I doubt it. She was the daughter of a British lord."

"Then she'll be buried at the non-Catholic cemetery."

It was the last thing she had expected him to say. But she had to be grateful he hadn't asked her questions she didn't want to answer.

"Could you tell me where that is?"

"I'll take you there."

"You don't have to do that."

"I know," he said, confusing her even more.

She didn't want him there, witnessing what might be another disaster. And she definitely didn't want him to be kind to her again, because it caused emotions that were not particularly helpful. But before she could tell him so he was already striding toward the bike.

She dashed after him, annoyed all over again by his arrogance and the renewed warmth pooling in her belly when he mounted the powerful bike and kicked the ignition pedal. Why did he have to look so sexy on the magnificent machine?

"Wait! All you have to do is tell me where it is." Having him there, watching and judging while she faced the demons she had been running away from for most of her life, would only make this harder.

"This is a one-time deal, Katherine," he shouted above the engine noise, as usual not giving her a choice. "Either climb aboard or you're on your own."

She glared at him, wishing she could tell him where to shove his devil's bargain. Unfortunately, she was way too tired and fed up to out-bully him. "What about the scooter?"

"It'll be okay until we get back here. We're not in Naples." He twisted the throttle, making the bike roar, then hooked the helmet off the handlebars. "Put it on, so we can get going. I haven't got all day."

She jammed the helmet on her head, muttering under her breath as she clambered aboard the bike. As they accelerated down the track in a spray of rocks and dust, she had to wrap her arms round his torso. The heady blast of heat shimmered down to her sex—which was still tender from last night's excesses—and it occurred to her that Jared's brooding presence at her mother's graveside wasn't the only reason why agreeing to this particular devil's bargain wasn't a good idea.

After a twenty-minute ride along the coastal road and through the narrow alleyways of Capri town to the hill-top cemetery, they found her mother's gravestone on a family plot in the far corner, nestled amid flowering vines.

*SALVATORE NAVARRO*
*Alexis Elizabeth Mary*
*In amore morì*

Katie ran her fingers over the names carved into the modest limestone slab, puzzled by the simplicity of the memorial. She had expected something much more elaborate for a woman who by all accounts had been a committed hedonist.

No dates, no insignia, none of the pomp and circumstance of the alabaster angels or marble Madonnas which adorned so many of the other graves. The stone just listed the name of the lover Alexis had died with, her own Christian names and the romantic Italian sentiment.

*Died in love.*

Emotions which Katie had kept hidden for so many years swelled in her throat. Vague memories, of sparkling green eyes so like her own, and an effervescent laugh, pushed at her consciousness.

Were those really memories of her mother, or simply projections which she'd clung onto as a child? She'd locked them away so long ago—ever since that miserable day when they'd buried her and the funeral had turned into a media circus—she would never know for sure. But, real or imagined, those memories blended with the anger and resentment which had colored her view of her mother for so long.

Alexis had been reckless and irresponsible, selfish and immature. It was hard to argue that point. How else could you explain the decision to abandon her own daughters? But after the intensity of what Katie had discovered in Jared's caresses—even the torturous pleasure of riding on a bike with him again to get to this very spot—she was finding it hard to continue to condemn all of her mother's choices. Was it really so terrible to want to live in the moment? And hadn't her mother paid a terrible price in the end for her impulsive pursuit of pleasure?

Letting out an unsteady breath, Katie placed the bunch of wilting wild flowers she'd picked at the roadside on top of the curved stone.

"I forgive you, Mom," she whispered. "Sorry it took me so long to come visit you again."

Brushing a tear from her eye, she stood up.

Jared was standing several yards away, his shoulder propped against the crumbling wall of a mausoleum, his hands tucked into the pockets of his ruined suit pants. The stance looked casual but the intent way he was watching her was anything but.

Her heartbeat kicked against her ribs and she wondered again why he had taken the trouble to bring her here. She swallowed down the stupid swell of emotion. It wasn't significant. He was probably just keeping an eye on her to make sure she didn't attempt to skip out on him. Running nervous fingers through her hair, she took a moment to look around the nineteenth-century cemetery which she hadn't taken the time to notice during their search for the grave.

She didn't recognize the place at all. She would certainly never have found it from her scattered memories of the day of her mother's funeral. It was such a beautiful spot, tranquil and ancient, the jumble of graves and tombs bisected by cobbled stone pathways and shaded by ancient oak trees which framed a breathtaking view of the sea from the cliffs above Capri's main town.

The musty smell of moss was layered with the ubiquitous spice of the citrus groves and the sweet scent of overripe figs from a nearby farm.

She breathed in a lungful of the sea air and felt the tangle of emotions that had gripped her ever since reading Jared's note begin to unwind.

Last night had been a mistake because it had meant so much more to her than it had to Jared but, as she walked past the graves, she felt lighter for having owned her own needs and desires. Unfortunately, as she approached him she was forced to acknowledge that those needs and desires were as strong, if not stronger, than they had been the night before. The low hum of arousal flared as his gaze roamed over her.

"All done?" he asked as he pushed off the wall.

She nodded, her throat suddenly thick.

To her astonishment, he took a hand out of his pocket and ran his fingertip down her cheek.

"You good?" he asked.

A lump formed in her throat and before she could stop it another tear dripped down her cheek.

"Hey, don't cry," he said, looking stricken.

She shook her head, trying to force down the wave of melancholy, but his concerned response only made it worse. Suddenly she found herself nestled against his shirt, her hands gripping his back and his arms tight around her shoulders as the tears she'd locked inside during all the years of her childhood and adolescent burst out.

Choking sobs rocked her, eventually subsiding into sniffs and shudders as the wave finally began to pass. He held her through it all, stroking her hair back from her face. He said nothing, but somehow his silence was so much more soothing than all the pointless platitudes spoken by well-meaning strangers which she remembered from that day. The musty masculine scent filled her nostrils and it didn't seem to matter anymore that she found it both comforting and arousing.

At last, he cradled her cheeks in callused palms and raised her head to look deeply into her eyes.

"You miss your mom a lot?" he asked as he wiped the last of the tears away with his thumbs.

She huffed out a self-deprecating laugh and tugged her face away, feeling weak, ashamed and hopelessly needy.

What on earth had the crying jag been about? She wasn't even sure where the tears had come from. And how could she have broken down in front of him? They weren't exactly friends.

"Hardly," she said. "I don't even really remember her. She walked out on me and Megan when I was still a baby." She sniffed, wishing she had a tissue handy. She probably looked a total mess. She noticed the wet patch on his shirt left by her tears. But then her gaze lifted to the strong column of his throat, and the wisps of dark hair revealed by the open collar of his shirt, and the heat that was never far away sunk back into her sex. She jerked her gaze to his face and managed a wobbly smile, trying not to obsess about how much she still wanted him. They weren't going to be doing the wild thing again. He'd made that abundantly clear in his note. And, however much her body might disagree, she still had at least some pride.

"Thanks for bringing me here," she said stiffly, going for polite and distant but getting breathless instead. "I needed to forgive her so I can finally begin to forgive myself for all the dumb stuff I've inherited from her."

*Such as my ability to fall in lust with totally inappropriate guys.*

His jaw tensed and she felt his withdrawal like a physical blow. She turned and walked swiftly down the path leading out of the cemetery, embarrassed by the revealing comment. Given his adversity to emotional attachments, her crying jag alone had probably been way too much information. But she'd gone less than five paces before strong fingers clamped on her elbow and he dragged her round to face him.

She steeled herself to see contempt—or, worse, pity. But instead, he looked guarded, while the pure blue of his irises glittered with an anger that for some strange reason didn't seem to be directed at her.

"What dumb stuff did you inherit from your mom?"

He shouldn't ask. He shouldn't want to know. Heck, he shouldn't even have offered to bring her here. And not just because riding a bike with her wrapped tightly around him had been agonizing.

But he couldn't seem to hold back the question any more than he'd been able to hold back his knee-jerk reaction to her tears.

Tears didn't usually impress him and they certainly had never made him want to offer comfort or support before now. But then he wasn't sure he'd ever seen tears as genuine or heart-wrenching as hers. Despite the initial show of bravado when he'd caught up with her on the road, she'd seemed so forlorn and fragile as soon as she mentioned her mom and her hunt for the grave. And that unwelcome feeling of responsibility had returned, compounded by the guilt from the night before.

Once he'd known she wasn't running away from him, the relief had been so huge it had been impossible for him to hold onto his temper. And then the exquisite torture of having her breasts flattened against his back and her arms banded around his waist, while the deep throb of the bike's engine rumbled up through his thighs, had done the rest.

He didn't know anymore whether it was the ongoing battle to control his lust or the unhappiness in her face which was driving the anger roiling in his gut but it didn't seem to matter.

With the lightly tanned skin of her cheeks reddened by her tears, she looked more vulnerable—and more determined not to show it—than he had ever seen her. He could feel the punch of her pulse against his thumb and knew he couldn't let her go until he knew what the heck she was talking about.

"You do know who my mother was?" she asked. "And the way she lived her life?"

Yeah, he knew, because they'd all been treated to a comprehensive assassination of the woman's character during Lloyd Whittaker's trial. The papers and bloggers had had a field day at the time with the stories of his ex-wife's many high-profile affairs which had been documented in salacious detail by the defense. He hadn't paid much attention because he wasn't interested in celebrity gossip and he didn't see what the heck Alexis Whittaker's checkered sex life had to do with anything, seeing as the woman had been dead for years. He still didn't, so he shrugged.

"I guess. But I don't see what that's got to do with you?"

Hectic color flooded her cheeks but she didn't relinquish eye contact. "Given the way I threw myself at you five years ago, and lied to you last night to get you to sleep with me, I would say the similarities between me and my mother are pretty obvious."

She tried to tug her arm free. He held on.

"Are you kidding me?" he said, stunned by the self-loathing in her voice.

"No, I'm not. You of all people should know that I'm just as much of a slut as she was."

She began to struggle in earnest, so he grabbed her other arm.

"Stop it," he said.

"Let me go, please."

"Not until you look at me, Katherine." He gave

her a gentle shake, unsettled by her distress, especially as he now knew he was the cause.

The wide pools of emerald green—so bold, so brave—sparkled with unshed tears, and the connection he'd denied so strenuously cracked the impenetrable wall he'd built around his heart.

"If you're a slut, how come you were a virgin last night?" he demanded.

He was furious, he realized, not just with Lloyd Whittaker—who he was sure had planted this nasty little seed in her head—but also with himself for helping it grow with his self-serving response to her sweet, artless seduction five years ago and his equally crummy note that morning.

"I tried to control myself, but with you I just couldn't anymore," she murmured. "And I never could."

His grip tightened at the reminder he was the only guy she had ever let touch her.

"That's why I came on to you when I was nineteen." Her gaze darted away. "And why I seduced you yesterday." She sighed, the sound so dejected the wall took another hit.

He tucked a knuckle under her chin and nudged her gaze back to his. "You wanna know why I got so mad with you when you tried to kiss me five years ago?" It was time to come clean about that much at least.

"I know why," she said. "Because the last thing you needed was some spoiled brat making your job even harder."

"Nope. I got mad because I wanted to kiss you

back so bad. And I knew if I did I wouldn't be able to stop."

Her eyes widened in stunned disbelief.

Damn, but she was more innocent than he'd figured. His blood surged south. Why that should make her even more irresistible, he didn't want to examine too closely.

"And you didn't seduce me yesterday, I seduced you." Which made his crummy note hypocritical at best.

Just like five years ago, he'd tried to slam the stable door shut after the stallion had bolted. And then put the blame on her.

*Great job, Caine. That makes you as much of a bastard as her old man.*

"But I don't understand..." she murmured. "If you wanted to kiss me that night why did you—"

"Shh." He pressed his thumb to her lips, then let it glide over her mouth.

He cradled her face in his palms. The quick catch in her breathing had him fixating on that lush mouth.

"How about I show you how much I wanted to kiss you?"

The tiny nod was all the permission he needed to cover her lips with his. The kiss was supposed to be gentle, an apology for the way he had treated her then and now. But when her mouth opened instinctively, the yearning to have her again shattered the last of his control and the kiss turned carnal in a heartbeat.

He plunged his fingers into her wild curls and she

arched against him, her tongue tangling with his as she surrendered.

God help him, but not even his knowledge of how vulnerable she was could stop him from taking what she offered.

Katie feasted on his kiss, rubbing her belly against the ridge of his erection. Arousal flared and need flooded through her. She sobbed her encouragement as his lips traveled down to the pulse-point in her neck.

One hot palm covered her breast and the tip engorged in a rush, painful in its intensity. She bucked, cried out. But then he tore his mouth away and stepped back abruptly.

"We have to stop," he said, the fierce regret in his face leaving her shaky and unsure. "I have to get back to work."

She folded her arms around her midriff and nodded. It was an excuse, and not a very good one at that, but as she took in their surroundings—the fresh flowers laid on the graves of the dead—she had to be grateful that he had brought them to their senses. Following him meekly out of the graveyard, she climbed back aboard the bike, her lips still stinging from the all-consuming kiss.

"You okay to get back to the villa from here?" Jared asked when they arrived at the place Katie had left the gardener's scooter.

"Yes." She nodded, so dazed she wasn't sure she

knew which planet she was on let alone how to get back to the villa. But after that soul-destroying kiss she needed time to get her equilibrium back.

"I'll see you tonight," he said, the husky tone only making her more unsure.

Katie touched her swollen lips as the bike sped off in a cloud of dust. She stood on the empty road until Jared had disappeared, her mind still reeling from the afternoon's revelations. And the devastating knowledge that he still wanted her as much as she wanted him.

# CHAPTER EIGHT

CONTRARY TO HIS promise that afternoon, Jared didn't show up for the evening meal, so Katie ate alone in her room and spent the rest of the evening immersed in her painting. But, instead of the landscapes she had worked on diligently after returning from the cemetery, she allowed herself the luxury of sketching the subject which had fascinated her for five years.

She moved to the villa's terrace after the staff had left for the night to make the most of the fading light as she finished the detailed line drawing and switched to oils.

The strength and beauty of Jared's naked body when he had stripped off in front of her came alive on the canvas and she came to a few important conclusions.

They were two young, healthy, unattached adults who desired each other. And they had two more days in this luxury villa to act upon that attraction. Now she had made peace with her mother and a legacy which she no longer felt responsible for, she didn't see why they shouldn't make the most of this opportunity.

Jared's failure to show up for dinner, though, suggested he was going to need more persuading.

Obviously, her inexperience and her ludicrous breakdown in the cemetery had made him believe she was a naive, clingy woman who wouldn't be able to abide by his "no emotional attachments" rule. While she had to admit she was still desperately curious about where that rule came from, and why he thought it was necessary, she needed to prove to him she could respect those boundaries if she wanted to take this afternoon's kiss to its logical conclusion.

Heat settled low in her abdomen and she pressed trembling fingers to her belly.

She absolutely did want to take it to its logical conclusion.

She caressed the lean line of his torso with her brush, finishing the final details on the portrait. She was twenty-four years old and she had denied herself the excitement and exhilaration of physical contact based on a lie Lloyd Whittaker had made her believe—that she was somehow responsible for her mother's sins.

It wasn't enough just to acknowledge that, or simply to own her desires, though. It was way past time she went out and demanded they be fulfilled.

Jared was here, available and obviously willing, and tonight she planned to show him that she too could be emotionally self-sufficient. He said he'd seduced her the night before—maybe it was about time she seduced him.

The thought thrilled and terrified her as she

packed away her paints and left the portrait to dry on the terrace. She showered and changed into a subtly sexy dress emblazoned with poppies and used some of the makeup samples the beautician had left to enhance her eyes and slick her lips. A pair of peep-toe sandals completed the outfit, which she hoped said "purpose and sophistication." And then she waited in the safety of her room late into the night, trying and failing to read one of the thrillers she had found in Jared's study, until she heard the low rumble of his bike.

She listened to the sound of the power shower going on in the adjoining suite and tried not to obsess at the thought of his body covered in steam and soap suds. His footsteps echoed in the room outside. Giddy anticipation intensified the ache in her abdomen as she stepped onto the terrace to find Jared wearing a clean shirt and dark jeans, his damp hair shining black in the moonlight.

His head whipped round as her heels clicked on the terracotta stone. And she released a tortured breath. He had the painting in his hands.

The thought that he had been studying her work had need and determination tightening the coil of desire. Sensation rippled over her bare arms, the citrus-scented breeze doing nothing to cool the hum of heat, as she walked toward him on unsteady legs.

"What's this?" he asked, lifting up the portrait. "Are you trying to shock my staff?" The tone didn't sound angry, just strained, but then she registered the lust-blown pupils edging out the pure blue of his irises. The fire blazed at her core, burning off some of the nervous tension skittering over her skin.

"They left for the night hours ago," she said. Gathering every ounce of her courage, she nodded at the portrait. "What do you think of it?" she asked, realizing his opinion mattered.

He stared at the canvas. Something flickered in his eyes, dark and tortured, and his Adam's apple bobbed.

The giddy pulse battered her collarbone.

"It looks romantic," he said, propping the picture back on the terrace table and burying his hands in his pockets. The edge in his tone made it clear the observation was a criticism, but instead of being cowed by his cynicism she felt suddenly empowered.

She wasn't the one running scared anymore.

"Do you really think so?" she challenged, stepping into his personal space and watching the rigid muscle in his jaw jump. "That's odd—I wasn't feeling romantic when I painted it." Not entirely true, because it was hard not to feel romantic in such a stunning place while painting such a ruggedly beautiful man, but that was surely just an aesthetic consideration?

"Oh, yeah? Then what the hell *were* you thinking?" he asked, his voice so husky now it was barely more than a croak.

"Isn't it obvious?" she asked provocatively, her own voice lowering several octaves as she sucked in a lungful of his enticing scent—pine soap and salty male flesh.

His brows slammed down, the muscle in his jaw going berserk as he lifted his hands out of his pockets and captured her waist.

"Don't tempt me, Katherine," he growled as he kept her at arm's length. "I'm trying to do the right thing here."

She lifted up on her toes, touched by the battle he was clearly waging with his conscience. "But this *is* the right thing," she whispered in his ear, then bit into the lobe.

Reaction shuddered through him and he swore softly as he yanked her the rest of the way into his arms. She sunk her fingernails into the short hair at his nape and gave herself up to the pheromones rampaging through her system as his mouth captured hers.

*To hell with Dario. To hell with being the good guy. To hell with doing the right thing.*

Jared thrust his tongue into the recesses of her mouth, gathering her exquisite taste. He cradled her hips and notched the heavy weight of his erection against the junction of her thighs.

He had spent hours holed up in his office persuading himself this wasn't going to happen again. That he couldn't risk sinking deeper into this emotional minefield. That he'd be taking advantage of her fragility, her vulnerability and her inexperience if he took what she offered again. He'd worked late into the night, forcing himself to stay away from her. But as soon as he'd walked out onto the terrace and found the picture she'd painted of him—those damning scars etched on his forearms, the naked need in his eyes, the aggressive erection captured in bold, unapologetic brushstrokes—he'd known he was lost.

Somehow, this wild, reckless girl had seen past the facade of success and sophistication to the broken man beneath, and she wasn't afraid of him.

She wrenched her mouth away, her body bowing back to increase the friction on her vulva. Her eager, artless response made the hunger claw at his insides.

She fumbled for his flies and her knuckles brushed the thick ridge which swelled and hardened in response. He sucked in a breath and captured her hand.

"Slow down, we've got all night."

Lifting her palm to his lips, he pressed a kiss to the base of her thumb.

Her breath hitched. "You're not going to change your mind?"

A gruff laugh rumbled out of his mouth, the surprised pleasure in her eyes humbling.

*If only I had a choice.*

He scooped her into his arms in answer to her question, enjoying her gasp as he carried her through the dark living room toward his bedroom.

They only had one more night. But, if they were going to do the wrong thing, he was going to make damn sure they did it right.

He made love to her as the moonlight glowed on her fragrant flesh, frantic and too fast at first, then slow and easy. He feasted on the soft sobs of her surrender as he brought her to peak countless times before finding his own release.

He held her afterward, their bodies still tangled together, the sweat drying on their skin and the musty scent of sex spicing the air as he listened to her breathing become slow and even. He should get up and carry her back to her own room, but his own limbs felt heavy and uncoordinated, too exhausted to move now the burning ache which had tortured him all day was finally satisfied. At least, for a little while.

She lay so trusting in his arms, her head nestled under his chin, her hand curled against his chest.

He tightened his arm around her slim shoulders. The unprecedented desire to wake up with her beside him in the morning scared him as his heart beat an erratic rhythm and he fought to keep his eyelids open.

# CHAPTER NINE

KATIE WOKE IN the darkness dragged from dreams of heat and desire to the sound of deep, unearthly sobs. As her eyes adjusted to the silvery light, she saw Jared's body curled in a fetal position beside her—his hands shielded his head, like a child trying to defend itself against a blow. It took her a moment to orientate herself and realize the heart-rending whimpers were coming from him.

"Jared?" She touched her fingertips to the bunched muscles of his shoulder. He flinched away from her touch. Sweat misted his clammy skin.

The whimpers turned to broken cries and her heart crashed into her throat as she made out the words he was muttering over and over again like a plea.

"Please stop… It hurts."

She acted on instinct, not knowing whether it was the right thing to do, but knowing she had to do something. Grasping his shoulders, she pressed her lips to the rigid muscles of his spine, then banded her arms around his wide chest and leaned over his shoulder and whispered in his ear.

"Jared, it's okay. You're safe. He can't hurt you anymore."

Violent shudders racked his body, the sweat dripping off him now and running in rivulets down the side of his face. She could see the pulse beating in his temple, hear the harsh rasps of his breathing and feel the screaming tension in the sinews of his arms as he wrestled with the nightmare.

Sympathy and compassion flooded her as he struggled with a terror so real and primal she couldn't begin to imagine what horror might have caused it. The broken cries turned to heart-rending sobs, the violent shaking making it hard for her to hold on to his sweat-slicked skin. But she struggled with him, trying to soothe, trying to help him break free from the chains of memory, whispering the same reassurances again and again.

"It's okay, Jared. I'm here. I'll keep you safe. You can wake up now."

He surfaced at last with a savage jerk and then stilled. His body went limp and she loosened her grip. They lay for a moment intertwined on the bed, his shoulders lifting and falling as he gulped in lungfuls of air, her hand pressed to his heart, absorbing the ferocious beating as it slowed.

Cursing softly, the words ripe with misery, he bolted upright on the bed, breaking her hold. With his back to her and his head bent, the sinews in his arms stood out as he gripped the edge of the mattress to steady himself.

He looked so alone in that moment. And so ashamed.

"Are you okay?" she asked, but the words seemed hopelessly inadequate.

"Yeah," he replied, his voice strained and hoarse. "Sorry I woke you."

Releasing his hold on the mattress, he rubbed his palms over the scars on his forearms, then massaged his knuckles into the damaged flesh as if trying to relieve the pain. Did the old wounds still hurt?

She flattened her palm on the rigid muscles of his spine, desperate to ease his suffering.

"Don't." He recoiled off the bed, as if her touch had burned him. "Don't touch me."

He stalked across the darkened bedroom to the open terrace doors. Naked, his body looked sleek and powerful limed by moonlight, as if he were a caged animal.

He turned, silhouetted in the moonlight, and she gasped at the sight of his arousal. He was fully erect, the evidence of his need thick and heavy and jutting out from his body at an obscene angle.

Heat fired through her system like molten lava as emotion closed her throat.

"You should go," he said, his voice grim with warning.

Beneath the threat she could hear the whisper of longing, the distress of that terrified child who had been hurt, who had needed comfort, and who had had no one. Her rational mind told her it was madness to think she could be that someone, but as the heat and desire mixed with the compassion in the milky darkness she knew she had to try.

She lifted the sheet, climbed out of the bed and walked toward him. The breeze skimmed over her bare skin.

His head lifted as she approached and she could feel the barely leashed hunger in his body as he straightened.

"I'm not kidding." He dragged unsteady fingers through the thick waves of hair. "You need to get the hell out of here…now."

She didn't stop, she didn't even falter, until she was standing in front of him, inches away, inhaling the addictive aroma of his skin. Absorbing the sight of him, both beautiful and terrifying.

"I don't want to get out, I want to stay here…" she whispered, her voice barely quivering, reminded of her wish from all those years ago. The molten heat gathered in her sex and burned through the final barrier around her heart. "With you."

Large hands shot out and grasped her upper arms in a bruising grip as he dragged her against him. He dropped his forehead to hers. Tension vibrated through him as the massive erection pushed against her belly and she understood the battle he was waging not to take what he so desperately needed.

"You don't know what you're asking for," he groaned, the tortured rasps of his breathing making her heart kick against her ribs. "I won't be gentle. I can't be."

She tugged her arms free and cradled cheeks rigid

with tension. She forced his tormented gaze to meet hers so he could see the truth in her eyes. "I don't care."

His need exploded with a raw groan and strong arms bound her to him. His kisses rained over her face, exploring her neck, sucking on the pulse point in her collarbone, feeding on her cries until he finally possessed her mouth with the forceful strokes of his tongue. She kissed him back, meeting him thrust for thrust.

He held her as his mouth claimed her breast, drawing the rigid nipple into the hot suction. She bucked against his hold, the heat arrowing down. Strong fingers found the slick folds of her sex, stretching the tight flesh. After the long love-making session the evening before, she flinched, but he didn't gentle his strokes. Instead he demanded more, his thumb circling the bundle of nerves with ruthless intent. She shattered, the orgasm battering her in fierce, undulating waves.

This was not the man who had made love to her for hours the night before with such skill and expertise, coaxing her to peak again and again. This man was raw, basic, brutal, his need primal and desperate, holding nothing back.

He shifted their positions. Her spine pressed against the cool glass of the terrace door as he lifted her. She wrapped her legs around his waist and clung to his wide shoulders, trying to steady herself, trying to prepare for the brutal invasion. But still her swollen flesh struggled to adjust as he lowered her onto the huge erection.

At last he was seated deep, so deep she felt impaled, not sure where he ended and she began. The waves of orgasm which had never really ceased began to batter her shattered body again as he grasped her hips and rocked.

She moaned, the hard, heavy thrusts forcing her back to another impossible peak with staggering speed. She clung to him, the only solid object in a stormy sea of exquisite pain, punishing pleasure. Her wild cries matched his hoarse shouts as he drove her past that final edge. And hot seed flooded her insides as he followed her over.

Jared glided on the shocking pleasure of afterglow, only vaguely aware of the tight clasp of her body and the dizzying aroma of sweet feminine arousal. Shudders racked his body and the sea breeze cooled the sweat on his skin.

But slowly he floated down from the high and awareness intruded…of his fingers digging into tender flesh. Soft breasts crushed against his chest. And the staggered sound of her breathing. He adjusted her weight, trying to relinquish the bruising grip on her hips, and heard the subtle moan. She massaged his length like a velvet fist and arousal pounded back into his crotch.

Shame engulfed him.

He drew out swiftly, before the need could overwhelm him, and he took her like an animal again.

As he placed her on her feet, she staggered and bitter regret tore into his chest. He'd treated her no better than a whore. He lifted her in his arms and walked on unsteady legs. He had to take her back to her own room. He couldn't be trusted. Why had he fallen asleep in her arms? How could he have allowed this to happen?

"Jared? Where are you taking me?" she murmured, piercing the thick fog of regret and recriminations.

"To your room. Where I promise you'll be safe from me."

Trembling fingers caressed his cheek and he was forced to stop and meet her gaze. He couldn't make out her expression in the darkness but the tender touch had his heart battering his ribs.

"You didn't do anything I didn't want you to do," she said, touching both his cheeks now as if pleading with him to believe her. "You do understand that, don't you?"

Her earnest statement nearly broke his heart. But he refused to accept her absolution. She didn't know she was worth so much more than he could ever give her. That she deserved a better man than he could ever be.

Hell, she probably even thought she was falling in love with him, and that would be the cruelest trick of all.

"Sure, but you must be tired," he said, the struggle to keep his tone casual and dismissive making his arms shake as he carried her into her room and placed her on the coverlet.

But as he went to leave she refused to relinquish her clasp on his neck. Pulling him back toward her, she placed a sweet, coaxing kiss on his lips.

"Really, Jared, you didn't do anything wrong. I enjoyed it," she said, her voice tremulous and unsure, but with the boldness of the girl he had come to know.

He reared back, breaking her hold as agony ripped through him—at the thought of all the things they might have had but couldn't, because of who he was and what he'd come from.

"Get some sleep."

He left the room without a backward glance. But he knew the image of her sitting on her bed in the moonlight, naked and vulnerable, her knees drawn up to her breasts as she tried to protect herself against the hurt he'd caused would haunt him for the rest of his life.

Katie wasn't a bit surprised to find Jared gone from the villa the next morning. She woke up feeling fragile, both physically and emotionally, after everything that had happened the night before. And she suspected Jared felt the same. She'd witnessed something she was sure he had kept hidden for a long time. The night terrors that she now knew were a regular occurrence had to come from some deep-seated trauma in his past.

But, while she was desperately sad at the thought of what he must have once endured to be so traumatized, at the same time she felt what had happened between them could only be a positive thing. He'd let down his guard last night, and so had she, and the connection between them had been strong, powerful and life-affirming.

This wasn't just about sex, it was about so much more than that. In so many ways they were kindred spirits. Hadn't they both been holding themselves back, keeping a tight rein on their emotions to protect themselves from hurt? Once she got a chance to talk to him properly, she would let him know that he could trust her to keep his secrets safe.

She went for a long swim in the pool and then had a leisurely breakfast on the terrace, hoping that he would put in an appearance at some point. By two o'clock she had finished all the landscapes she had been working on the day before and was considering tracking him down at the resort's business center when a call arrived from Megan.

They spoke for over an hour, and although Katie was careful not to divulge the details of her affair with Jared she knew her sister suspected something when she revealed that she had visited Alexis's grave the day before. And also that she had made the decision to return to New York with Jared.

But she resisted Megan's careful probing. She couldn't talk to her sister before she spoke to Jared. She needed to keep her optimism under control. Even though she was certain they'd reached an important turning point the night before, they'd only slept together twice. What they had was hardly even an affair let alone a relationship and she had to be careful not to get ahead of herself. His distance last night after they'd made love had been clear and unequivocal. It had felt like a blow at the time but, after a solid five hours' sleep and some time to think and reflect, she was sure he was just wary of the emotions they'd both unleashed.

He was a cautious, guarded man who had good reason to be scared of emotional attachments. It made sense that he would leave it up to her to take the next step, especially as she suspected he felt guilty about taking her virginity. Which was of course nuts, but he was a guy.

After hanging up the phone she called the business center. But once she finally got through to Jared's executive assistant, he informed her that Signore Caine was conducting a meeting with the heads of his security teams and would return to the villa by four o'clock.

Galvanized into action, Katie hunted through the wardrobe Donatella had selected. She tried on three different outfits before finally settling on a tomboyish combo of Capri pants, camisole and linen shirt. Nerves skittered over her skin when she heard the deep rumble of the motorbike pulling into the car port at four exactly. She waited on the terrace, trying not to let all the thoughts and feelings from last night overwhelm her.

That said, it was still impossible to quell the rampant beat of her pulse when he stepped out into the sunlight. In his suit pants, and tailored white shirt, a thin tie neatly knotted at the collar, he looked every inch the business tycoon—composed, commanding and detached. A million miles away from the man she had seen the previous night and was very much afraid she was already halfway in love with.

"Hi, how are you?" she asked, then wanted to kick herself. Seriously, could she sound anymore inane after the enormity of what they've been through the night before?

But he barely even blinked before replying. "Good. I can't stay long. I just thought I'd come back and check that you're good with tonight's travel arrangements?"

She was so surprised by the pragmatic tone it took her a moment to register what he was saying. "What travel arrangements?"

He loosened his tie and undid the first button of his shirt. "I'm heading back to Manhattan tonight on the company jet. Your passport arrived from the British Consulate an hour ago, so you can accompany me if you want."

She didn't have any objections, of course. She had already made the decision to return home. And that wasn't really because of him and what had happened between them. It was mostly to do with her visit to her mother's grave. Yesterday she had finally made peace with her mother's legacy and come to terms with why she had spent so long running away. Plus, Megan and Dario were expecting her. But there was something in his tone, in the controlled expression, that had her nerves tangling in her stomach into a knot of anxiety.

He was behaving as if last night had never happened. As if the connection she'd felt didn't exist.

Had she completely misconstrued the significance of those moments?

"It has occurred to me," he continued in the same impersonal, businesslike tone, as if she were one of his employees, "that while Dario and I had agreed you would travel back to New York with me when your passport arrived, the final decision should be yours."

Part of her realized she should be pleased with this development too. He was giving her a choice, giving her the agency she'd wanted four days ago when he'd insisted on bringing her to Capri in the first place. But the whisper of impatience in his tone and the blank expression on his face didn't feel good. It felt like a blow. A mortal blow to the foolish hopes and dreams she'd nurtured during the day.

"I'm happy to go back with you tonight," she said. "I spoke to Megan this afternoon and I've realized it's the right thing to do. That I'm ready to start putting my life back together again."

He nodded, the movement oddly stiff. But his expression remained carefully blank, making the thoughts whispering through her head seem even more melodramatic and misguided.

"Let the staff know you're coming with me and they'll pack for you." He planted one hand in his pocket, his stance so casual and unconcerned now she knew she wasn't imagining his withdrawal. "I can't hang around. I've got too much to finish up here, and then I have a meeting in Naples before we fly, so I'll meet you at the airport."

She jerked forward as he turned to leave. "Wait, Jared." She touched his arm and he swung round, dislodging her fingertips.

"Yes?" he asked, one eyebrow raised as if she were an inconvenient distraction.

"Shouldn't we talk? About last night?" she managed, pushing the words out past the lump forming in her throat.

He let out a deep sigh. "Yeah, I guess we should. I had planned to leave this until we got back to Manhattan but it's probably better to handle it as soon as possible." There was no mistaking the strain in his voice, but even so she felt the tiny bubble of hope. So she hadn't imagined something had happened.

But then he said, "Things got out of hand last night and I didn't use protection." He sunk both his hands into the pockets of his pants and studied her as if she were a particularly rare bug under a microscope. "Is that going to be a problem?"

The blush burned her neck as the hope burst, leaving the familiar feeling of insecurity and inadequacy in its wake. "I…I don't think so," she mumbled, realizing she should have given the situation some thought herself. But, after everything else, it hadn't even occurred to her.

"I'm guessing that means you're not on the pill?"

"No, I'm not, but…" The question hadn't sounded harsh, judgmental or condemnatory. It had simply sounded pragmatic. But, even so, it reminded her of all the times Lloyd Whittaker had made sneering judgements about her intelligence and common sense. And her reply got caught in her throat.

"But what, Katherine?" he coaxed.

"I'm due in a few days. It's unlikely that there'll be any consequences," she blurted out, feeling hideously exposed.

He nodded again, the stiff line of his shoulders visibly relaxing. "Okay, that's good. But if there are any consequences you need to let me know. And we can deal with them together."

"But…won't we be seeing each other once we get back to New York?" she asked, unable to extinguish the final flicker of hope.

He frowned and she suddenly felt like the naive girl again who had once thrown herself at him. "I don't think that's smart, do you?" he said, the finality in his voice the final blow.

"I don't understand, I thought… Your nightmare—I…" She bit back the words, scared she might cry and make an even bigger mess of things.

"I'm sorry you had to witness that," he said, his expression ruthlessly controlled. "And I'm sorry I got rough afterward. But you're an extremely desirable woman and you offered."

He was making the encounter sound insignificant, even a little sordid. And it hadn't been, at least not for her. But what did she really know about sex, about relationships? She was so stupidly inexperienced.

Had she blown everything out of proportion, read meaning into his actions that simply wasn't there?

He touched a fingertip to her forehead and drew it down the side of her face. Her breath seized in her lungs as the brutal tug of yearning ripped through her.

"I thought you understood," he said, his voice gentle. "When we got into this, I wasn't looking for anything more." He tucked the stray strands of hair behind her ear and she felt like a child again, looking for affection she didn't deserve.

She nodded, absolutely devastated as he tucked his hands back into his pockets and walked away from her.

The trip back across the Atlantic was agonizing. The distance he'd already established was compounded by the curt, businesslike attitude Katie remembered from their encounters five years before. She had to be grateful that his executive assistant was returning on the private jet with them and Jared spent most of the time discussing business while she slept fitfully on the bed in the back of the cabin. He said goodbye to her at JFK, insisting again that she should call him if there were any consequences from their recklessness. But she noticed he didn't even glance back as the private car Dario had arranged drove her away from the terminal.

# CHAPTER TEN

KATIE DROPPED HER paintbrush in the cup of turpentine. Blowing out a breath, she rolled her shoulders to ease tight muscles and studied the composition. She'd been up well before dawn that morning, unable to sleep for another night, compelled to finish the picture. Jared stared back at her, his face full of naked hunger, his beautifully sculpted body gleaming with sweat and taut with arousal.

Awareness blossomed in her sex and she winced.

This was the fourth picture she had done of him in the last two weeks. In fact, Jared was pretty much the only subject she seemed compelled to paint. She would never be able to sell any of the work—even if she could be convinced to let anyone else look at it. But, having analyzed and reanalyzed every moment of their brief time together on Capri, she couldn't seem to stop trying to paint her way to a different outcome.

She'd had her period three days after returning to Manhattan and, while on one level it had been a relief, on another it had devastated her. Especially when it took her two days to get up the courage to text him with the news—writing and rewriting the message in the vague hope that it might begin a dialogue between them—only to receive a five-word reply.

Thx for letting me know.

She had become obsessed with Jared and their microaffair and she needed to stop. He couldn't have been clearer about his feelings. Or rather his lack of them. She had caught him at a vulnerable moment, thrown herself at him, and he had been unable to resist her. Then she had blown their four-day encounter completely out of proportion as a way of validating her behavior.

But somehow she couldn't seem to throw off the draining lethargy of the last few days and the ludicrous thought that something wonderful had been within their grasp and she might never get over the loss.

She'd spent the first week after getting back from Capri trying to work him out of her thoughts. After setting up a website and scouring for commissions, she had managed to secure a gallery showing in Brooklyn, regular work doing designs for a greeting-card company and—with a little help from Dario's connections—had sold her Capri landscapes to an Italian travel giant for use in their logo. The money she had earned had been just enough to pay the rental deposit on a tiny apartment in Queens, so she had been able to move out of Dario and Megan's beautiful townhouse.

But, since moving in four days ago, she hadn't been able to maintain that work ethic—partly because she'd been running on so little sleep, partly because she couldn't concentrate on painting anything but Jared. But mostly because all the misery, and the endless reappraisals of every second they'd spent together, had crowded back in.

The might-have-beens had begun to torture her. All those questions which she had never even been able to ask. What had happened to Jared to give him those terrible nightmares? Could she have reached him if they'd had more time? Why had he been so determined not to see the possibilities?

She sighed and draped a cloth over the unfinished painting. The first hurdle was getting over the obsessive urge to paint erotic portraits of the man.

She switched her attention to the design on her work station which she was actually being paid to do.

The door buzzer sounded, cutting through the noise of a delivery lorry idling in front of the Korean grocery store below.

She lifted the brush out of the turpentine to clean it with one of her rags as she walked across the narrow room and checked the peephole.

Anxiety churned in her stomach. What was Megan doing here, with her toddler son Arturo perched on her hip and a stubborn expression on her face?

Katie considered pretending she was out. But then Megan's gaze fixed on the peephole.

"I can see your shadow over the hole, Katie. So stop messing about and let us in. I just spent twenty minutes trying to find a parking spot."

Katie spent as long as she possibly could undoing the chain and the four locks on the door while searching for her happy face. The one she had last worn in Jared's bed.

She might as well not have bothered, because as soon as Megan walked into the apartment she gave her a deliberate once-over and then frowned.

"Katie? I don't believe it—you've actually lost more weight. And you look as if you haven't slept for weeks!" she said, repeating the familiar refrain which had helped drive Katie out of her sister's home.

Arturo began to fuss, obviously picking up on the distress in his mother's voice.

"Hey, Artie, how's tricks?" Katie sent her nephew her brightest smile and lifted him out of his mother's arms, ignoring her sister's plaintive plea.

This was the problem with having people who loved you—they couldn't stop butting into your life.

The baby grasped a hunk of Katie's hair in grubby fingers, easily distracted—unlike his mother.

"I'm serious, Katie, you look dreadful. What is going on with you?"

"Gee, thanks, sis."

Arturo wriggled out of her arms so Katie put him down on his sturdy little legs. In such a tiny apartment, there was a limit to how much damage he could do without her or Megan running interference, Katie reasoned. He toddled off, using the sagging sofa to keep himself upright, raring to get into mischief.

"Do you want a cup of tea, then?" she asked, heading for the apartment's galley kitchen. "Or are you just here to tell me how awful I look?"

Keeping half an eye on her son in that way all mothers adopted instinctively, Megan followed Katie into the kitchen and opened the fridge door.

"I'll have tea if you'll have something for breakfast." She slammed the fridge closed. "Which is going to be next to impossible, seeing as you have nothing in your fridge except coffee."

Katie put on the kettle, feeling harassed. "I have a grocery store downstairs that sells everything from bagels to radish kimchi when I need it."

"Then why aren't you using it?" Megan asked, her gaze on Katie's waistline.

"I've been busy, Meg, I'm not starving myself." Or, not intentionally anyway. It was just hard to locate her appetite when all she could seem to think about was Jared.

"Is this something to do with Jared—and the reason he's been out of New York ever since you guys got back from Italy?"

Katie's head jerked up but the mention of Jared's name had color flaring across her collarbone.

"No." The word choked out on an unconvincing huff.

Where had he gone? And why had he left? She

had made a point of not going to any events with Dario and Megan or paying attention to the gossip columns since she had returned. She wanted to keep a low profile so she didn't draw any of the unwanted attention from the press she had gone to Europe to avoid. But she also knew she couldn't bear bumping into Jared or seeing him escort some other woman to the VIP events. She had also made a point of not asking Dario about his friend, mostly not to alert her brother-in-law to the fact she was desperate for even the slightest bit of news about him.

"Something happened between you two. I know it did." Megan's gaze fixed on her like a Rottweiler's. "Because you have both been acting weird ever since you got back. I've never seen you so subdued—"

"It's called being a grown-up," Katie interrupted, feeling more dejected than ever. Had she made the nightmares worse, she wondered, by stirring things up while they'd been together?

"And Dario is worried about Jared," Megan continued, ignoring Katie's comment. "He won't answer any of his calls and he's been staying up at his place in Vermont even though he usually only goes there during the winter-time to ski."

Katie searched for something coherent to say that would deflect her sister's concern. Even though she had never managed to get to the bottom of the friendship between Jared and Dario, and why Jared felt so indebted to her brother-in-law, she was positive he would not want Dario to know about their affair. But the urge to tell Megan was almost overwhelming—

because all she could think about was Jared, alone in his cabin, torn apart by the nightmares with no one to comfort him. Dario needed to go up there and make sure his friend was okay.

She was just about to say so when an almighty crash had both women jumping. Megan dived out of the kitchen first and hoisted her son into her arms. Luckily Katie's easel hadn't landed on top of him, but her paints were scattered across the floor. Katie arrived in time to see Megan pick up the canvas of Jared which had fallen facedown.

Megan turned to her, jiggling her fractious son on her hip, and sent her a smile full of compassion and understanding as she held up the painting. "Well, this explains quite a lot."

The blood rushed to Katie's head, her knees buckled and she sat heavily on her tiny couch, knowing she and Jared were totally busted. Now all she had to do was explain the unexplainable to her inquisitive sister.

"I think you should go and see him, Katie. Not Dario," Megan said, the urgency in her voice starting to give Katie a headache.

"I can't do that, Meg. I think I may have messed things up enough already for him."

She'd explained everything to Megan. It had been a precondition of her sister agreeing not to contact Dario. They sat on the sofa, Arturo sound asleep next to them after his near-death experience.

"Why would you think that?" Megan asked. "This

isn't more of that ridiculous guilt-fest you had going over Mom is it?"

Katie sat up, glad when her head didn't start aching more. She thought about it for a moment, then shook her head. "No, I know I'm not responsible for Mom leaving us. Or for the fact Lloyd Whitaker blamed us both for Mom's infidelity. Jared helped me to see that. But I feel like I took advantage of him when I slept with him that last time. I knew he was vulnerable and I…" The blush scolded her cheeks. "I sort of seduced him."

"Katie, he's a grown man with a great deal more experience than you."

"I know that, but what if those terrible nightmares were somehow triggered by me and something I did? I lied to him about my virginity. I didn't tell him because I think I'd always wanted him to be the one, after that stupid crush I'd had on him when I was nineteen. Don't you see I tricked him? And it really rattled him. I know it did."

"You didn't trigger those nightmares," Megan said with complete certainty.

"How do you know that?"

Katie could see knowledge in her sister's eyes and realized that she knew answers to the questions Katie had never been able to ask. Even so, she didn't want to press—what right did she have to invade Jared Caine's privacy even more?

Megan stared at her for a long time and then sighed. "I probably shouldn't be telling you this, because Dario told me in confidence, and I don't think it's something Jared wants people to know, for obvious reasons. But I think..."

"Then you mustn't tell me. I'm pretty sure I mean nothing to him and I wouldn't want to—"

"That's where I think you're wrong," Megan interrupted. She grabbed hold of Katie's hands and squeezed. "You're a bright, strong, beautiful, brave, passionate and extremely talented woman, Katie. I know that, Dario knows it. I think Jared figured it out while you were with him. The only one who doesn't know it is you."

Katie's heart bobbed into her throat at the sincerity in her sister's voice.

Megan studied Katie's fingers, stained with turpentine and oil paint, and ran her thumbs over the nails Katie had chewed in the last few weeks.

"What do you know about Jared's past?" she asked. "Did you ask him about it?"

Katie shook her head. "We were only together four days and he's not a man who it's easy to ask personal questions of." She gulped down the guilt that she'd ever assumed she even had the right to ask. "All I know is that he comes from humble origins because that's what I've read in the gossip columns."

Megan rubbed Katie's knuckles and then raised her head. "Not humble. I think 'horrific' is probably a better description."

"Horrific, how?" Katie asked, all the empathy and concern for Jared that she had tried so hard to deny for the last two weeks spilling over into her voice.

"I don't know the specific details, neither does

Dario. But this is what I do know… Dario caught him trying to pick his pocket. He was only fifteen, in and out of foster homes, mostly living on the street. Dario took him in that night because he was obviously starving, but sharp and quick, and Dario…" A pensive smile tugged at her sister's lips. "Well, Dario knows what it's like to have nothing and no one too. Dario contacted the authorities the next day and helped make sure that over the next few years Jared had all the support he needed. Both financially and, as far as he would accept it, emotionally too."

Tears stung the back of Katie's eyes at the thought of how alone Jared must've been and how important Dario was to him. No wonder he had been willing to do anything Dario asked of him. Including getting stuck for four days in a luxury villa with a woman who did nothing but annoy him.

"Your husband really is one of the good guys, isn't he?" Katie said, feeling even more foolish for the reservations she'd once had about Dario when Megan had first become engaged to him.

Megan's smile blossomed. "Yes, he is, but don't tell him that. His head is quite enormous enough already."

Both sisters laughed, but Katie's felt strained.

"The thing is, Katie," Megan said, her smile dying, "Dario told me Jared had those night terrors the first night, when he was staying in Dario's apartment. Dario paid for him to live in a residential home for street kids until he reached maturity, because he couldn't settle with a foster family. But he had those crippling nightmares at the home too. I have no idea where they come from. And neither does Dario. And Jared refused to do more than a couple of sessions with the home's therapist. So the fact he even let you comfort him is, I think, a pretty big deal."

Megan eased a tendril of hair behind Katie's ear, reminding her poignantly of the last time Jared had touched her. "And the fact he seems to have run off to some remote cabin in Vermont to brood and lick his wounds seems even more significant. Jared has spent most of his life protecting himself. It's extremely hard to win his trust. Dario managed it, but only after years of friendship, and that clearly has its limits if he can't talk to Dario now about this. You seem to have won his trust in a matter of days."

"Did I?" Katie wanted to believe it with all her heart, but she didn't want to hope. "I'm not sure I did. I thought there was a connection there, something to build on, but I don't know if he did."

"Well, there's only one way to find out," Megan said, her voice as sure, steady and reassuring as Katie remembered it being throughout their childhood.

Stupid to realize, she thought as gratitude made her ribs ache, that she had always believed she didn't have a mother because Alexis Whitaker had abandoned them as children, when she actually did. And always had.

"What way's that?" Katie asked, almost scared to ask but even more scared not to act on the hope bubbling back into her chest.

"You'll have to go and ask him."

A tear-soaked chuckle escaped Katie's lips as her sister wrapped her in a hard hug. When they finally broke apart, Megan said, "I'll get Dario to lend you the company helicopter to get to Vermont."

Katie didn't want to mooch off her billionaire brother-in-law, but pride was going to have to take second place to the need to confront Jared before she lost her nerve. "Okay, but what is Dario going to make of the fact that Jared and I slept together? I don't want to mess up their friendship."

"You won't," Megan said, her eyes shiny with emotion. "I'll explain everything to Dario. He'll probably freak out; he's not super-evolved when it comes to understanding love either. But I know how to handle him. And I should be able to get everything organized by tomorrow morning."

"But that's twenty-four hours away. I don't know if I can wait that long to see Jared," Katie said, her impulsiveness returning in a rush.

And to think she'd once thought that was a flaw.

But Megan wouldn't be swayed, insisting that Katie wasn't going anywhere until she'd had at least twelve hours' sleep, and Megan had witnessed her eating a three-course meal. With or without radish kimchi.

# CHAPTER ELEVEN

KATIE WAS GRATEFUL for her sister's mother-hen tendencies at noon the next day when the De Rossi Corp helicopter landed beside the lake on Jared's ten-acre property. Thanks to the sleep and sustenance Megan had insisted upon, the nervous tension in her stomach was just about manageable, instead of catastrophic.

Nestled amid a grove of towering spruce and pine trees, a strikingly modern cedar-wood house stood beside a traditional redwood barn. The large wraparound porch looked out onto the placid waters of the lake, in stark contrast to the rolling waves of anxiety pounding Katie's stomach.

Taking a deep breath she jumped out of the helicopter and waved goodbye to the pilot.

Jared's tall figure appeared from inside the house. Dressed in worn jeans and a checked shirt, his feet bare, his hair rumpled and with a coffee mug in one hand, he should have looked relaxed. But as she made her way toward him through the field of wild grass, the noise of the departing helicopter drowning out the thundering beat of her heart, she could see from his rigid stance he was anything but.

She took her time, absorbing the beauty of their surroundings and trying to get straight in her head all the things she needed to say to him. She could see she might have underestimated the task ahead of her when she arrived at the porch.

His usually clean-shaven jaw was shadowed with a week's growth of beard, the angular lines of his face even leaner than she remembered, and his brows were drawn down in a heavy frown over the piercing gaze that had remained locked on her every step of the way. Arousal stirred as his gaze roamed down and then returned to her face, the bold appraisal setting alight every millimeter of skin en route. His jaw tensed, and heat and desire flickered in the deep aquamarine of his eyes.

She resisted the answering tug of desire in her abdomen, knowing if he could he would use it to distract her from the conversation she had come here to have.

The noise and wind caused by the helicopter slowly faded into silence until all she could hear was the plaintive cry of a cormorant, the peaceful lap of the water against the dock at the back of the house and the frantic beat of her own heart.

Unlike the lake, Jared looked about as peaceful as a ferocious grizzly bear who had been woken from its midwinter hibernation.

Katie swallowed past the obstruction in her throat.

If he had come to Vermont to recover the control he'd lost that night in Capri, it didn't appear to have worked. Her heart jolted in her chest, compassion tangling with anxiety and nerves in the pit of the stomach.

What was she doing here? Had she made a terrible mistake? What if Megan was wrong about her ability to heal this taciturn and tormented man's heart?

Had he been suffering with those terrible nightmares all this time?

She tucked her fingers into the back pockets of her jeans to disguise the trembling. "Hello, Jared, how are you?" She fought to keep her voice firm and even and betray none of the emotion that was ripping apart her insides.

Maybe he didn't want her help, her sympathy or concern—and would rather die than admit he needed it—but she intended to give it to him anyway.

He studied her, taking a long gulp from the coffee cup. She watched the column of his throat bob as he swallowed, the motion sending another shaft of heat through her system.

At last he placed the cup on the porch rail and folded his arms across his chest.

"What are you doing here?" he said at last, his voice so rusty she could tell he hadn't spoken to anyone in days.

"Checking up on you. Dario's worried about you—we all are."

His brows flattened and the muscle in his jaw jumped. Grasping her arms, he dragged her toward him, pulling her up on tiptoes. "If Dario's sent you here to give me some of your unique sexual healing," he sneered, his eyes bright with arousal and fury, "then I'll take it." He held her close, his breath whispering over her lips, the promise and provocation of that sensual mouth so close to hers the heat spiraled down to her core. "Otherwise, get lost."

He released her abruptly and she stumbled back. But as he turned to stalk back inside the cabin she bolted forward and grabbed his arm.

Catching him unaware, she was able to haul him round to face her. The crude invitation had been meant to repulse her. She understood that. And suddenly a fury of her own burned deep in her chest.

"You think I'm scared of you and how much I want you? I'm not." Or, not anymore. The arousal surged. "I'm willing to own it. Are you?"

She saw his control snap and he grasped her arm to haul her into the cabin.

"Great, let's own it together," he said as he dragged her through the living area and up a flight of slatted stairs to a bedroom on a mezzanine platform under the cabin's slanted roof beams.

Cedar-wood eaves framed a large bed while the glass back wall afforded a stunning view out onto the lake. But Katie barely registered any of that, all her attention concentrated on the man in front of her as he grabbed the back of his shirt and dragged it over his head. Excitement charged over her skin as he wrestled her out of her clothes. Buttons popped and fabric tore in his urgency—but, instead of scaring her, his desperation empowered and excited her. Within seconds they were both naked. She felt giddy with need as they collapsed onto the bed together.

The last of his anger unraveled into a storm of longing as he jerked her thighs apart and buried his face between her legs. She bucked off the bed, broken sobs torn from her throat. Locating the swollen nub with his mouth, he swirled his tongue over the heart of her, and then sucked, dragging the orgasm forth with ruthless efficiency.

She was dazed, still coasting on the brutal wave as he rose above her and angled her pelvis, cradling her bottom in firm hands.

The huge head of his erection pressed at the swollen folds of her sex. Hunger and torment, like that of a starving man, etched his face as his eyes met hers. But he held back even though the need to take her vibrated through his body.

"You really want this?" he asked, his voice full of a desperate despair.

She cradled his cheeks and kissed him hard on the lips before whispering in his ear, "Yes. Yes, I do."

He buried the huge erection to the hilt in one powerful lunge then moved in hard, heavy thrusts. His seed exploded inside her moments later, his shout of release so full of agony her heart felt as if it might burst out of her chest.

She lay with him in her arms, caressing the thick waves of his hair, his heart thundering against hers as he collapsed on top of her.

Eventually his pulse slowed, beating in deep

thuds in time with hers. The rhythm of his breathing hitched as a heavy sigh rumbled against her ribs.

"Are you okay?" he murmured, lifting off her and studying her face as he touched her cheek with his thumb. "Did I hurt you?"

She could feel the tender spot between her legs where he was still firm inside her, the sublime aches and pains from the urgency of his love-making, even the stinging abrasion on her thighs from the rough stroke of bearded cheeks.

But she shook her head, because it didn't hurt. However inexperienced she was, she had never been fragile. And the only pain she could feel right now was his.

Forcing himself to get off her before he collapsed on top of her, Jared walked over to his discarded clothes and yanked on a pair of boxer shorts. He felt weary to the bone.

Holding onto the dresser, he ducked his head.

"I just made love to you without a condom again," he said, unable to look at her. He was no better than an irresponsible kid. The same irresponsible kid who had once been reduced to using sex as a substitute for affection.

He'd done it deliberately, he admitted to himself, sick with disgust—the desire to get her pregnant all part of the madness which had gripped him ever since he'd walked away from her at JFK. Hell, ever since he'd picked her up on the road outside Sorrento. Maybe even before that. Did this all-consuming need to brand her as his in the most basic way possible track all the way back to that night when she had looked at him with such yearning—and for one brief, shining second he'd wanted it to be real?

"I'm now on the pill," she said in a tremulous voice.

His head swung round, elated and appalled at one and the same time, especially when she sent him a tentative smile and said with complete sincerity, "I didn't want there to be anything between us if I ever got to make love to you again."

"Hell, Katherine." He scrubbed his hands over his face and dragged his fingers into his hair. "What am I going to do with you?"

Her honesty and openness, her bravery and generosity, crucified him and made him feel like even more of a coward. He'd been rough, uncontrolled, just as he had been on their last night together. And she had taken everything he had to give her and reveled in it. But still he knew he'd defiled her innocence, taken advantage of a situation she would never understand.

He wasn't worthy of her, could never be worthy of her, and he would have to tell her why not. He was going to have to reveal all the sordid details of his past, his childhood, or she would never realize how wrong she was about him.

But first he needed a beer.

Leaving her on the bed, he trudged down the open staircase and walked to the kitchen on the far side of the living room. Opening the double-wide refrigerator, he pulled out a bottle and rolled it across his forehead, hoping the frosty condensation would cool the flush burning his skin.

He popped the cap and took a long draught.

He heard the soft pad of her bare feet on the granite flooring. She had followed him into the kitchen, just as he'd known she would. Because she had more bravery in her little finger than he had in his whole damn body.

He turned to lob the cap into the trashcan and had to bite down on his lip to control the renewed kick of desire in his crotch.

She had donned his shirt. It swamped her slender frame, reaching almost to her knees. But as she walked toward him the tails shifted, giving him an uninterrupted view of lacy panties and those long legs which had been wrapped so securely around his waist as he'd pounded into her like a man possessed.

He concentrated on taking another swallow of the cool brew.

Maybe he was possessed. Possessed by her. Was that why the nightmares hadn't stopped? Why they'd plagued him every night in his dreams in the two weeks since he'd forced himself to walk away?

He'd come to Vermont to escape them. But the cabin had been too silent. Too solitary. The hard physical tasks he'd set himself—repairing the broken shingles on the barn, chopping enough wood to survive a nuclear holocaust—hadn't taken the edge off his hunger. And seeing her in his kitchen, the residual hum of desire still flowing through his veins, now he knew why.

Ever since he'd escaped the horrors of his childhood he'd always been self-sufficient, at his most content in his own company. He'd never thought he was lonely, because he'd been determined never to need anyone but himself.

But after a few short days sharing a villa with her, and only one night sharing a bed with her, she'd managed to invade every corner of his consciousness. She'd captivated him, not just with her body but with her personality—that heady mix of boldness and vulnerability, innocence and bravery.

He took another long lug of beer but the cold, malty taste did nothing to moisten the arid dryness in his throat.

"Why do you want to be with me, when you don't know me?" he finally forced himself to ask.

"Because I do know you," she said, so simply and so directly he wanted to weep. "We're a lot alike. We spent so long running from our feelings that we'd forgotten how to feel. How to trust—not just others but ourselves too. I don't want to be that person anymore. I want to stop running. Because I've discovered it's better to feel everything than to feel nothing at all."

He let his head drop and grasped the bottle.

"I'm not like you," he said, bracing himself to answer the questions he knew would come next—and which he would no longer be able to avoid. "I'm not the guy you see on the surface. I've done things… had things done to me…that I can't change. And it makes me unfit for the kind of human habitation you're talking about."

Surely the way he'd taken her—not once, but twice now—proved that beyond a shadow of a doubt? The animal instincts, the desperate need to claim her, to mark her as his, came from a fear which he'd never been able to overcome—that deep down he knew he deserved to be lost in the dark forever.

"Are those things the cause of your nightmares?" she asked softly.

But it wasn't softly enough to stop the shame which he had kept buried inside for so long from careering to the surface like a runaway train and smashing the last of his composure to smithereens.

Katie watched his head jerk up and saw the naked pain in his eyes. Emotion trembled in his arms as he braced them against the countertop, drawing her gaze to the wounds on the tanned skin of his forearms.

"What happened to you, Jared? Can you tell me?"

He dropped his chin to his chest, the dejected nod almost more than she could bear.

"When I was a little kid it was just me and my mom." He began talking in a flat monotone, as if he was reciting a story that had happened to somebody else. "We lived in a tiny walk-up in Brooklyn. She held down two jobs. We were barely getting by from pay check to pay check, but I didn't know that, because she made sure I had everything I needed. Then she hooked up with a guy called Bannon. He was the local bookie. It was cool at first. I liked him. I'd always wanted a dad, someone to play ball with. And he made a fuss of me. Called me 'son.'"

He shrugged, the movement brittle, the sheen of sweat visible on his chest despite the hum of the air conditioning.

"First time I saw him hit her, I persuaded myself it was her fault. He was a jealous guy, he loved her—and he was screaming at her, saying she had flirted with some other guy. I was ten years old, I didn't understand adult relationships, and it was easier to blame her than to admit the guy I hero-worshipped was a monster.

"By the time I was eleven, he had gotten over his jealousy, because he had her turning tricks for him. She was tired all the time and strung out on the drugs he got her hooked on. She wasn't my mom anymore. She had become a shadow of the woman she'd once been. I still made excuses for him. Still tried to make it right in my head. But I knew it wasn't.

"Then one day, not long after my eleventh birthday, which my mom had forgotten about, he told me he was taking me to see the Yankees to celebrate. Even though I was wary of him, I believed him. I was so excited on the way there. He bought me a hotdog and a soda and a ball-cap. We watched the game. I'd never been to the stadium before and I was high on the whole experience. The Yankees snatched it in the final innings. But when we headed to the subway to go home, he took the wrong train. We got off at a stop I didn't recognize, in the Bronx. My mom wasn't much good to him anymore he told me, but I…I could make some dough for us both. 'You're a good-looking kid,' he said. 'And small for your age. I know guys who will pay a pretty penny for a piece of that. And I'll give you a cut.' I threw up the hotdog. Even at eleven years old, I knew what he meant."

Katie covered her mouth, the horror story unfolding making her yearn to take him in her arms. But she knew if she touched him too soon he would break. As he continued to talk, though, her heart broke for that little boy.

"I kicked up a fuss and he swiped me, hard across the face. It was the first time he'd ever hit me. I tried not to cry, but I was so scared. The best day of my life had suddenly turned into my worst nightmare. He picked me up and carried me kicking and carrying on to this house with neon lights over the door. Once he got me there he took his cigarette and burned my arm a couple of times, until I stopped shouting and screaming and I was just numb. Then he locked me in there and told me he'd be back and I better behave or there would be more of the same. I kicked and carried on when he came back and he burned me some more. It went on for days. Until there wasn't any fight left in me. That's when…"

She saw him swallow and knew this was the worst of it. She swallowed too, her own stomach raw. "He brought some guy back with him and he raped me. It hurt like hell. But I didn't even cry—because I couldn't. When it stopped, and they left, I lay there for a long time looking at the neon blinking over the door. It hurt to move, but some part of my mind knew that if I stayed there I'd end up like my mom, a shell of myself. So I broke the window and climbed through. And then I just ran. The cops caught up with me and stuck me in the system, but every time they put me with a new foster family I ran again. And I just kept on running until the night when I decided to palm Dario's wallet in Greenwich Village and he caught me. But a part of me never got out of that room. And it never will."

A sob choked out of Katie's throat and Jared's head rose, the blank expression turning to bone-deep regret.

She brushed away the tears she hadn't even realized were streaming down her cheeks. "It's not your fault. What he did to your mother. What they did to you. You do know that?"

"My rational mind wants to believe that. Dario paid for therapy while I was in the home. And the guy told me that. But whenever I go back to that room in nightmares, I hate myself more each time. Don't you see what that nightmare is telling me? I can't be the guy you need, Katherine. Not in the long term. Because I'll always be that scared little kid, trying to get out of that room."

The relief was palpable as she realized how wrong he was about himself. All she had to do was make him see it. He wasn't scared of loving her, he was simply scared of not loving her enough.

"But that's not true, Jared. You got out of that room, and you helped me get out of that room too.

You didn't just face down your own demons, you helped me face down mine. What if the nightmares aren't telling you you've failed, but that you succeeded?"

"How can that be true when I just took you like a madman again?"

She stepped toward him, seeing the anguish in his eyes. Sliding her hand into his, she lifted the back of his fingers to her cheek. "No, you didn't. You gave me a choice. A choice I wanted to make. A choice I enjoyed."

He stroked a fingertip down her cheek to tuck the unruly hair behind her ear. "That's just the sex talking, Katherine. Good sex. Great sex. But it's just sex. You don't know that, because I'm the only guy you've ever had sex with."

She sniffed and a small smile tugged at her lips as she realized how wrong he was. "True," she said, suddenly feeling euphoric. "But you're also the only guy I've ever fallen in love with."

He looked shocked and wary. "Why would you love me when I'll always need you so much more than you can ever need me?"

"That's simply not true, Jared. I need you more than you can ever know. I did five years ago. And I do now."

He shook his head, still unconvinced, still so unsure. "You had a crush on me five years ago. That's all."

"Maybe it was a crush, but even then there was something there, a connection that neither one of us could deny. You looked at me and you saw me. I was just a bratty kid, desperate for attention and affection, but you made me feel like so much more than that. And even then you protected me, from myself most of all."

"I was protecting myself..." he said. "Not you. I called you a spoiled brat. I slapped you down. I..."

"Because you were cornered, Jared. And at that moment I *was* being a spoiled brat. I didn't understand what that connection was then, but I do now." She cradled his face and kissed him with all the love in her heart, then whispered against his lips, "I wasn't mature enough to love you then, but I am now."

He eased her back, the torment in his eyes tempered by need.

"I *want* to love you," he said. "But what if I'm not capable of love?"

She could hear his fear and suddenly she knew that a part of the young boy who had seen the best day of his life turn into the worst still lurked inside him. That he was scared to grab the golden ring in case it turned to dust in his hands.

But the only way to make the fear go away was by showing him he had the power to defeat it.

"Don't you see? Just *wanting* to love me is enough," she said. "If you're ready to stop running and try. Are you?"

It was a risky question. Their whole future rested on the answer, but the euphoria and hope built in her chest because she could already see the answer in his eyes as he studied her.

"I'm not sure I have a choice," he murmured. "Because the one thing I am sure of is I'm not strong enough to walk away from you again."

The smile spread across her face and filled her heart to bursting. "I'm going to take that as a yes."

He cupped her cheeks in his palms and rested his forehead on hers as his fingers caressed her nape.

"You do that," he growled, before cupping the back of her head and bringing her lips to his in a mind-numbing kiss, full of the promise and possibility of bone-deep yearning and unconditional love.

# EPILOGUE

"WHAT'S GOING ON down there?" Jared squinted, the light from the early-evening sunshine making it hard to focus on Katherine and her sister who stood on the pool terrace below the De Rossis' villa on Isadora.

But something was going on, because Katherine had just wrapped her arms around Megan. And was hugging her hard enough to bruise.

He'd been on the island for a couple of hours, having arrived by helicopter that afternoon from a conference he'd been attending in Rome. But, after a brief kiss when he'd arrived, Katherine had been busy helping Megan put the kids to bed and he'd been trapped helping out Dario on the outdoor grill.

He'd been waiting for Dario finally to ask him what he guessed his friend had wanted to ask him for months now. What the heck did he think he was doing dating his sister-in-law?

Because Dario knew what Jared had been and what he was capable of. And Dario must have serious doubts, because he still had serious doubts himself.

Not what he was doing with Katherine, but what the heck she was doing with him.

She was beautiful, talented and smart. But, more than that, she was the center of his universe—had been for twelve months now. Twelve months which had gone by in a flash of color and light and sensation—of long, hot nights, and short, contented days whenever the two of them could get away. He from the demands of his business, and she from her growing career as an artist.

But Dario had kept silent, talking about pretty much everything but the huge elephant between them that now felt as if it were sitting in the pit of Jared's stomach.

Dario glanced up from flipping lamb steaks on the grill like a pro—and grinned as he directed his gaze to the terrace below. "I expect she is telling Katie our news."

"What news?" Jared asked.

He'd been desperate to see Katie. They'd been apart for three days and the hunger for her that never eased was stronger than ever—but he knew it would be hours before he could touch her again.

Katherine had moved in with him six months ago at his insistence. So he knew this reckoning was long overdue—but he had an answer ready for when Dario finally came at him.

He loved Katherine. She'd brought something into his life that he thought he could never have, could never deserve. Not just great sex, and lots of it, but stability and companionship. He'd never realized how lonely he was until he'd had her waiting in his loft apartment when he got home in the evening. Usually she was wearing one of his old shirts, her hair and arms covered in flecks of paint as she finished off some commission or one of the pieces for another of her shows.

Maybe he owed Dario his life. But he didn't owe the guy his happiness. Or Katherine's. And she was happy. He'd made sure of it.

He'd wanted to push for more now for a while. Wanted to ask Katherine to marry him. He wanted his ring on her finger. But he hadn't brought the subject up because he didn't know what the heck to say. How even to get it said. He wasn't a romantic guy and, every time he tried to get his head around how to make the proposal, it started to hurt. And he knew the truth was, it had nothing to do with the logistics of a proposal—how hard could that be? A good wine? A nice location? Make yourself look like a jerk? Job done.

What really made his head ache and his heart hurt was the thought that if he pushed, if he asked for that one more thing, that ultimate commitment, the dream state he'd been living in for a year would dissolve in front of him and turn out to be exactly that—nothing more than a dream.

He'd even spoken to the damn therapist about it. The woman Katherine had found and eventually badgered him into seeing—which had helped with the nightmares.

Dr. Carlton had told him the fear of rejection was in his head, part and parcel of the baggage he'd been carrying for years from his childhood abuse. Baggage that he was finally starting to shed with her help, and Katherine's. But it seemed neither one of them could help him with this. Because every time he thought of going down on one knee, of asking Katherine to be his forever, that little kid who'd sat terrified and alone waiting for the axe to fall lurched out of hiding.

"We are having another *bambino*." Dario's voice, filled with contentment and no small amount of masculine pride, broke into Jared's musings.

The shaft of envy was so swift and so sharp it took a moment for Jared to muster up the required smile.

"No kidding, man?" he said. He slapped Dario on the back, trying to sound pleased, when all he could think about was Katherine heavy with *his* kid. That slim, coltish body ripe in pregnancy…

The longing hit him hard. Katherine would make a terrific mom. But how could he ask her to bear his child when all the fates were stacked against him making an even halfway decent dad?

"That's great," he added, because Dario was looking at him with a curious smile on his face that he didn't like.

"You don't sound sure," his friend said.

"You and Megan make great parents—what's not to be sure about?" he asked, but comprehensively failed to keep the sting out of his voice.

"Right," Dario muttered, concentrating on lifting the steaks off the grill and laying down some strips of eggplant that his housekeeper had marinated before leaving the island with the rest of the staff for a day off.

Jared's temper and frustration spiked. He didn't want any bad blood between them. But suddenly he was through tiptoeing around this situation. "Listen, if you've got a problem with me and Katherine being a thing, why the heck don't you just come out with it?" he demanded, his temper warring with his frustration—and a choking sense of vulnerability.

Dario tensed, and stopped distributing the eggplant to spear him with a look that could only be described as disgusted. "Yes, I have a problem with your thing," he snapped back.

The elephant plummeted to Jared's toes.

Dario was the only man he had ever respected. The only man whose opinion mattered to him. And he was Katherine's only male relative. If Dario told him all bets were off in this relationship, it would hurt. And it would end their friendship. Because he wasn't giving her up. Not now. Not ever.

"When are you going to stop fooling about and claim her properly?" Dario added.

"What do you mean *properly*?" Jared demanded.

"You must marry her, of course, give her your name. She deserves that much, don't you think?"

"You *want* me to ask Katherine to marry me?" Jared asked. Was that approval he could see in Dario's eyes alongside the flash-fire spark of temper?

"Why would I not?" asked Dario, and it was his turn to look confused.

The tension in Jared's stomach dissolved, along

with the crushing fear that had dogged him through most of his life. That he would never be good enough, strong enough, finally to escape from that room forever. And he laughed.

"I don't suppose you've got any suggestions for how to make it happen, have you?" If Dario was cool with him and Katherine making their thing permanent, why not get the guy's help?

Dario flipped one of the eggplant slices and smiled. "My only suggestion is to get her pregnant."

"That's kind of drastic, isn't it?" Jared wondered, knowing he couldn't expect to have all his wishes come true at once.

"It is." Dario's lips quirked. "But it worked for me."

"I have some news too." Katie grinned as she let her sister go, not sure that anything could be more perfect than Megan's announcement.

"Oh, my God." Megan gripped Katie's hands and squeezed. "Don't tell me Jared's finally popped the question?" she asked.

Katie's smile faltered, but only slightly. And she shook her head.

It had been an ongoing topic of conversation for months now between her and Megan. Sort of a running joke, really. That after badgering her endlessly to move in with him officially and let her apartment go in Queens—even though she had already been spending most of her time at his place—Jared had stalled on the obvious next step. For six months.

But Katie wasn't really bothered about the prospect of a proposal. It would be romantic and wonderful to plan a wedding but she couldn't feel any more secure in his love than she did already. And she was more than prepared to propose to him if the need arose. The only reason she hadn't was because she thought they both needed more time to adjust to the newness, the wonder, of this relationship. Jared still had the occasional nightmare. He was still battling those demons that had been embedded in his psyche after the traumas of his childhood. She didn't want to ask something of him he wasn't yet ready to give. She was more than happy to wait.

Or she had been, until two days ago, when everything had changed.

And the time to be free and easy and relaxed about this relationship, the honeymoon period of allowing themselves all the space they needed to adjust to the realities of this commitment, had suddenly run out.

She touched a hand to her stomach, determined to be excited by the discovery she had made the morning after Jared had left for Rome. This had to be a good thing. She was going to make it a good thing. So much had changed since that first pregnancy scare—surely his reaction wouldn't be the same now? It couldn't be. But still a part of her wished it hadn't happened like this, without the proper planning and consideration.

Although, she had to see the irony of the situation—that the original wild child, the woman who had once reveled in her own impulsiveness, was now having impulsiveness thrust upon her due to a stupid mishap with her contraceptive pill.

"Katie, oh, my..." Megan pressed her hand over Katie's, having picked up on the instinctive gesture. "You're not...?" She looked speechless for a moment, but her eyes misted with emotion.

Katie nodded, her own eyes stinging.

Megan wrapped her arms around her in a tight hug. "This is so terrific. We'll be as big as houses together. Jared must be overjoyed."

Her sister said it with such confidence, but even so the whispered fear Katie had refused to acknowledge for two whole days—while she'd held off telling Jared over the scratchy Internet connection to Rome—shouted across her consciousness.

*But what if he's not?*

"I haven't told him yet," she admitted as Megan finally released her.

"Why not?" Megan asked.

"Well, I..." She breathed, trying to get her excuses in order—not easy under her sister's all-seeing eye. "There hasn't been a good time. I only found out a couple of days ago and he was in Rome. And...well."

"Well, when *are* you going to tell him?" Megan demanded, lasering through all Katie's excuses to get straight to the point.

"I thought I'd tell him tonight, once we're in bed together." Because sex always made things simpler. And she knew he was ravenous for her, because she'd seen the hunger in his eyes when he'd kissed her after his arrival, and she was just as ravenous for him.

Surely if she just popped out the information while they were both floating on a wave of after-glow Jared wouldn't freak out?

But even she could hear the question in her voice.

Megan frowned. "Katie, you do know he worships the ground you walk on, right?"

"I know, but…this is completely unexpected. And unplanned. We haven't ever talked about children. I'm on the pill. Or I was. But I had a stomach bug three weeks ago, and I must have thrown up one or something. It's low dosage so it's—"

"Katie, calm down." Megan gripped her arms to halt the stream of way too much information as all Katie's insecurities came babbling out. "You're blowing this out of proportion."

"How can you blow a baby out of proportion?" Katie retorted, appalled at her sister's cavalier attitude. "This is a *baby*, Megan!" she said, just to be sure her sister had heard her, as the magnitude of the problem really sank in. "It's a person. A human being. Who is going to be relying on me and Jared one hundred percent."

Megan's lips kicked up in a grin. "I know what babies are, Katie. I've had a couple myself and I'm about to have another."

"Yes, but you and Dario are so good at being parents. You're naturals. I'm not sure Jared and I are. We're not prepared for this. As overjoyed as I was when the stick turned blue, I…" She stopped and took a moment to draw a careful breath and admit her greatest fear. "I'm scared it might be too soon to take this step. I'm not sure either one of us is ready. But even though my head is telling me that, my heart knows I can't give Jared a choice." She pressed her palm to her belly again. Even if it was still only a collection of cells, the baby felt so real to her already. "Because I want to have this baby, so much."

"Shh, Katie." Megan's smile didn't falter as she cradled Katie's face in her palms and wiped away a tear Katie hadn't even realized had slipped down her cheek. "First off, no one is ever prepared. Even if they think they are. And Dario and I certainly weren't," Megan said. "You've already gone one better than us by managing to be together for a whole year before this happened, instead of one night," she added, huffing out a self-deprecating laugh.

"I know, but...what if he doesn't want to have it, Meg?"

"Honestly?" Megan said, looking so much surer than Katie felt. "I think once he gets over the initial shock he'll be overjoyed too. Jared's a tough guy. He's survived a lot in his life, like Dario—a baby is not going to phase him in the least once he gets used to the idea. And it's obvious whenever we see you two together..."

Megan took a breath. "Which isn't nearly often enough for my liking, by the way," she added, going the full big sister. "That you mean the world to him. And I'm sure this baby will too. Frankly, I think a much bigger problem is going to be dealing with his desire to keep you housebound once he finds out about your condition. It's taken me three pregnancies to get Dario's protect-at-all-costs gene under control and we're still working on it. Plus, I've got a sneaking suspicion Jared might be even worse—given his choice of profession."

"Really?" Katie asked, the surge of hope making her heart bob into her throat.

"Yes, really... But there's only one way to find out for sure," Megan said, and Katie was reminded of a year ago, in her tiny apartment when her sister had given her advice once before on her relationship with Jared. And look how that had turned out!

"Don't tell me." Katie put up her hand, the excitement now at least as big as her fear. "I just need to ask him."

"Bingo," Megan said, and they both laughed.

Katie's laughter had died by the time she and Jared were saying their goodnights to her sister and Dario. The meal had gone by in a blur—her trepidation and nerves almost as huge as her anticipation. Something had changed between Jared and Dario. They'd obviously had some kind of clearing of the air while she and Meg had been down by the pool, because as the four of them prepared the casual meal and sat down together to feast on the delicious combination of lamb steaks and a range of *antipasti* Megan and their housekeeper Maria had prepared earlier it was obvious the two men were much easier in each other's company than they had been since she and Jared had started dating.

Even so, the tension had mounted between Jared

and her every time their eyes had met across the table. The hunger in his gaze, that concentrated need, had sparked a need of her own as he'd watched her with feral intensity and she couldn't resist the opportunity to tease him by making a production of consuming the succulent tiramisu.

She let the desire flow through her—knowing it was him and not the wine intoxicating her, of which she'd only taken a small sip—as he clasped her hand in his and all but dragged her through the terraced gardens, down to the guest house nestled amid a grove of wild flowers. Pulling her into the dark room, he slammed the door and pressed her back against the wood.

"I have something I need to ask you," he said in a low, urgent tone. And the tension in her tummy twisted. Did he know? Had he guessed?

But then his hand grasped her leg and hooked it over his hip, bringing the thick ridge of his penis into contact with her clitoris. The pressure felt glorious, and frustrating, separated by his suit pants and the damp fabric of her panties. "But I have to have you first."

"Me too," she said. Gripping his head in both hands, she urged him on, buoyed by the sound of ripping lace and then the sibilant hum of his zipper, deafening in the darkness.

"I can't wait," he growled against her neck, plunging his fingers into the slick folds to test her readiness.

She bucked against the door as he touched the

very heart of her, tightening the urgent spiral that had been torturing her for days, ever since he'd left. "Then don't," she said.

Grasping her hips in rough hands, he lifted her. She moaned, the guttural sob raw and basic as he impaled her in one solid thrust. She rode the thick invasion, powerless to limit the speed or depths of his thrusts as he forced her toward that bright, shining ledge, ruthlessly stroking that place deep inside.

In only a few thrusts, the coil tightened unbearably and then shattered, sending blistering shards of light through her body as his grunt of fulfillment matched her cry of release.

She was still floating on afterglow, the erotic smell of sex and sweat mingling with the light fragrance of sea and citrus and the deliciously familiar scent of him—the erection still firm inside her—when he lifted his head and pressed a hard, fleeting kiss to her lips.

"You have to marry me," he whispered.

"Jared…" She stroked his face, the rough stubble making sensation skitter back to her core where he was still lodged inside her. The shock at his words made her almost as giddy as the sudden spurt of joy. He hadn't asked, of course, he'd told her. And the circumstances could hardly be described as romantic.

"Give me an answer, damn it," he said, sounding so bossy, and desperate, the joy leapt in her chest, overtaking the last of the fear she'd lived with for two days.

What was wrong with her? Megan was right.

They loved each other. To distraction. He'd want this baby simply because she did. And any reservations they had, any fears, they'd get over together, like they had everything else.

But somehow she couldn't help teasing him.

"I didn't hear a question," she said.

He swore softly, pressing his face into her neck, kissing the pulse point tenderly and then easing her off him. For a moment she felt bereft and shaky, her knees going liquid, but he held her as they adjusted their clothing. And finally pressed a kiss to her hair as he wrapped strong arms around her.

"I'm sorry. That's got to be the worse proposal any woman ever got. I've been thinking about asking you for months and, when I finally get up the guts to do it, I mess it up."

*Months?* He'd been planning this for months? The giddy leap of joy became all-consuming.

"It's not the worst at all," she said, taking pity on him in her euphoria. She drew back so she could look up into his face. "I think every woman should demand a mind-blowing orgasm right before a proposal."

He let out a strained laugh. "Ya think?"

"FYI, the answer to the question you never actually asked is yes."

He jerked in her arms and her heart melted into a puddle at her feet at the thought he had ever believed this might be in doubt.

"For real?"

She nodded.

The wayward tears stung the backs of her eyes

again when he pressed a kiss to her forehead and sighed. "Thank God."

She cradled his face to pull him back, so she could make out his expression better in the moonlight streaming through the guest house window. "But I've got something to tell you too."

"What?"

She took his hand and pulled it down to press his large palm against her belly where their baby grew, the one she already knew would be loved and cherished by its parents the way the two of them never had been.

"We'll have to get a move on with the wedding if we don't want a gate crasher."

His head rose, and for the first time ever, even in the half-light, she could see every emotion cross his face. His expression was completely unguarded. Shock, concern and a flicker of complete and utter panic.

But then the scar on his top lip bobbed as his mouth stretched into an awed smile.

His hand stroked her invisible bump as he stared down at her abdomen. "How long have we got?"

"Eight months."

He drew her into his arms. The sure, solid beat of his heart pounded against her ear as warm hands stroked her back, but he didn't say anything, so she had to ask.

"Are you okay with this?"

"I'm overjoyed," he murmured against her hair.

"And scared to death. Does that answer your question?"

"Absolutely," she said, the width of her own smile giving the full moon a run for its money. "Because that's exactly how I feel."

His hands paused for a moment on her back. "But from now on rough sex against a door is off the table." He held her hips to draw her back, a stern frown marring his brow. "You should have told me about junior before we did that..."

*And so it begins*, she thought.

"I'm pregnant, Jared. Not an invalid."

He hoisted her into his arms. "Shut up, Katherine, and do as you're told for once," he said as he carried her into the guest-house's bathroom as if she were as breakable as glass.

But as he made slow, agonizingly gentle love to her, the water cascading down their naked bodies, she let him have it his way, just this once.

Once he had coaxed her to a devastating climax, they collapsed together into the lavish guest bed. He held her securely in his arms as he dropped into sleep. There would be no nightmares tonight, she knew as she stroked the damp locks of his hair, heard the deep, contented murmur of his breathing—and planned the best way to jump her new fiancé first thing tomorrow morning so she could show him rough sex against a door was never off the table.

But she couldn't keep her eyes open, her sated body beckoning her into dreams—bright, beautiful, wonderful dreams full to bursting with all the possibilities, the challenges, the joys and intense, all-consuming love for him and their children the months and years ahead would hold.

* * * * *

*If you enjoyed*
*CAPTIVE AT HER ENEMY'S COMMAND,*
*why not explore these other stories by Heidi Rice?*

*THE VIRGIN'S SHOCK BABY*
*VOWS THEY CAN'T ESCAPE*
*PUBLIC AFFAIR, SECRETLY EXPECTING*

*Available now!*

Available April 17, 2018

## #3617 KOSTAS'S CONVENIENT BRIDE

by Lucy Monroe

Kayla's boss Andreas must marry! After she experienced the incandescent pleasure of his touch, his proposal is everything she's dreamed of. But dare she risk her heart to become a convenient wife?

## #3618 THE VIRGIN'S DEBT TO PAY

by Abby Green

Merciless Luc will hold Nessa captive until her brother's debt is settled. And when undeniable attraction overwhelms them both, Nessa's innocence is the real price to pay!

## #3619 CLAIMING HIS HIDDEN HEIR

*Secret Heirs of Billionaires*

by Carol Marinelli

Seduced then dismissed by her demanding boss Luka, Cecelia's hiding a secret—their daughter! But when Luka uncovers her deceit, there's no escaping the consequences of her passionate surrender...

## #3620 THE INNOCENT'S ONE-NIGHT CONFESSION

by Sara Craven

Zandor awakened Alanna to an unknown sensuality—but shocked at her own passionate response, she fled! When Zandor reappears, this time she can't run from the sizzling intensity of their connection...

HPCNM0418RA

## #3621 DESERT PRINCE'S STOLEN BRIDE

*Conveniently Wed!*

by Kate Hewitt

To reclaim his country, Zayed *must* wed. He steals away his intended...only to realize shy Olivia is the wrong woman! But with such heated chemistry between them, do they want to correct their mistake?

## #3622 HIRED TO WEAR THE SHEIKH'S RING

by Rachael Thomas

As Jafar's temporary wife, Tiffany is perfect. Yet this convenient arrangement for his crown leads to passion! Is their craving enough to make Tiffany more than just the sheikh's hired bride?

## #3623 SURRENDER TO THE RUTHLESS BILLIONAIRE

by Louise Fuller

Luis is shocked to learn the beautiful stranger he spent one scorching night with has also been hired by his family! He whisks Cristina away to uncover her ulterior motive...and rekindles their incendiary desire!

## #3624 PRINCESS'S PREGNANCY SECRET

*One Night With Consequences*

by Natalie Anderson

Damon can't resist a sensual encounter with a captivating guest at a royal masquerade. But he's shocked to discover she was actually Princess Eleni—and now she's carrying his baby!

---

SPECIAL EXCERPT FROM

***"Did you forget to tell me about my baby?"***

*Buttoned-up PA Cecelia Andrews's resignation released her secret raw desire for her demanding playboy boss, Luka Kargas. Now, one year after his callous dismissal, Cecelia's hiding an even greater secret—their daughter! She'll* never *let coldhearted Luka make her daughter feel unwanted. But when Luka uncovers her deceit, there's no escaping the consequences of her passionate surrender…*

*Read on for a sneak preview of*
Carol Marinelli*'s next story*
*CLAIMING HIS HIDDEN HEIR*
*part of the* **SECRET HEIRS OF BILLIONAIRES** *miniseries.*

"We were so hot, Cecelia, and we could have been good, but you chose to walk away. You left. And then you denied me the knowledge of my child and I hate you for that." And then, when she'd already gotten the dark message, he gave it a second coat and painted it black. "I absolutely hate you."

"No mixed messages, then?" She somehow managed a quip but there was nothing that could lighten this moment.

"Not one. Let me make things very clear. I am not taking you to Greece to get to know you better or to see if there is any chance for us, because there isn't. I want

HPEXP0418

no further part of you. The fact is, you are my daughter's mother and she is too young to be apart from you. That won't be the case in the near future."

"How near?"

Fear licked the sides of her heart.

"I don't know." He shrugged. "I know nothing about babies, save what I have found out today. But I learn fast," he said, "and I will employ only the best, so very soon, during my access times, Pandora and I will do just fine without you."

"Luka, please..." She could not stand the thought of being away from Pandora and she was spinning at the thought of taking her daughter to Greece, but Luka was done.

"I'm going, Cecelia," Luka said. "I have nothing left to say to you."

That wasn't quite true, for he had one question.

"Did you know you were pregnant when you left?" Luka asked.

"I had an idea..."

"The truth, Cecelia."

And she ached now for the days when he had been less on guard and had called her Cece, even though it had grated so much at the time.

And now it was time to be honest and admit she had known she was pregnant when she had left. "Yes."